THE TREASURE OF JUNIPER JUNCTION

To Melton Pritchard Snyder — inspired by the summer I spent on a graduate fellowship from the University of Pennsylvania at Point of Pines, the University of Arizona archaeological field school on the Apache Reservation.

THE TREASURE OF JUNIPER JUNCTION

A Novel

Emily Cary

Emily Cary

iUniverse, Inc.
New York Lincoln Shanghai

The Treasure of Juniper Junction

Copyright © 2006 by Emily Cary

All rights reserved. No part of this book may be used or reproduced by any means, graphic, electronic, or mechanical, including photocopying, recording, taping or by any information storage retrieval system without the written permission of the publisher except in the case of brief quotations embodied in critical articles and reviews.

iUniverse books may be ordered through booksellers or by contacting:

iUniverse
2021 Pine Lake Road, Suite 100
Lincoln, NE 68512
www.iuniverse.com
1-800-Authors (1-800-288-4677)

This is a work of fiction. All of the characters, names, incidents, organizations, and dialogue in this novel are either the products of the author's imagination or are used fictitiously.

ISBN-13: 978-0-595-41164-1 (pbk)
ISBN-13: 978-0-595-85521-6 (ebk)
ISBN-10: 0-595-41164-9 (pbk)
ISBN-10: 0-595-85521-0 (ebk)

Printed in the United States of America

Chapter 1

Tracy was admiring the spectacular Arizona vista when her reverie was distracted by the sound of an approaching car. Several hundred yards distant, near the edge of the Apache settlement, it stopped by the roadside memorial. Like so many impromptu memorials erected along highways or at cross-streets to commemorate a loved one's abrupt and cruel passing, this one was bedraggled, ravaged by weather and neglect.

From her vantage point atop the remains of an ancient pueblo, Tracy watched the driver, a woman, climb out and retrieve a basket from the back seat. Kneeling on the ground, she began refurbishing the site. Soon fresh flower pots encircled the cross. Satisfied, the woman swept the refuse into a trash bag and stood to assess her work. Tracy shivered. It was impossible to mistake the haughty carriage, the lithe, pampered body of the woman crossing the road to toss the bag into a garbage bin. Even in her later years, she retained the characteristics that set her apart.

Tracy rose, pondering the wisdom of making her presence known. A feeble try later, she acknowledged that her voice was not powerful enough to cut through the incessant wind sweeping across the plain. Convinced that their meeting could do little more than churn up bitter memories of an event best left to history, she stood motionless while the woman returned to the car, made a K-turn, and drove away.

Exhaling, relaxed once more, Tracy returned to her perch. Turning toward the western sky, she drank in the panorama. Thirty years had not changed the sweeping prairie, the mountains that encircled it, and the air pungent with aromatic pine.

She gazed down at her hands, smiling ruefully. Time had its way with the mortals who tarry briefly on this earth. Still, she could not complain. Her body, firm and athletic despite her age, could easily pass for one far younger. As for her own accomplishments, she was proud of her highly regarded travelogues that evolved from the exotic climes where her husband's work took the family.

In the intervening years, Tracy had surveyed the ruins of countless ancient civilizations and enjoyed the hospitality of both primitive tribes and contemporary royalty. And yet nothing surpassed the satisfaction of returning to the past and discovering that sometimes one must take that detour to clear the gateway to the future.

Soon the hot pink sky would give way to the approaching twilight. Stars would appear, one by one, celestial rhinestones studded on ebony velvet. Filled with delight and apprehension, Tracy entered her store of precious memories. Once again, she was the young woman about to commence an adventure, unable to imagine the treasure she would find along the way and the secret awaiting discovery. Both would define the rest of her life.

The plane emerged from the clouds. Below was the barren surface of the Southwest desert, a parched land born of searing heat. From the cabin window, Tracy Reynolds studied regimented circles of green, the distinctive irrigation pattern favored by ranchers. Infrequent structures emphasized the desolation. The visual contrast to her lifelong surroundings amid the skyscrapers and hubbub of New York City was a shock.

Had she been too rash in walking away from her comfortable, though sometimes boring, relationship with Ken?

They had dated on and off for five years, never committing themselves, yet grateful that the other was a phone call away, a dependable companion at the latest Broadway show or on a Sunday drive to the beach. If Tracy's mother had not died unexpectedly, the lessons she drilled into her daughter might have prevailed. A frequent participant in the benefits and concerts that defined the city's social life, Mrs. Reynolds had been raised amid wealth and prestige. It concerned her that Tracy's peers, young women whose own mothers goaded them to marry up a notch, did exactly that. Determined that her daughter would join the social whirl, she was overjoyed when Tracy began dating Ken, a rising stock broker from a family boasting a line of blue-blooded ancestors.

Tracy continued seeing Ken after her mother's death. Like many teenagers, she had rebelled against standards she regarded as outdated and irrelevant, often dating young men whose social and financial positions failed to meet family approval. Her campaign to express her individuality continued into college where she chose an unlikely major for a young woman being groomed to prevail in polite society. But even before graduation, her headstrong tendencies were tempered by the death of a parent and the reality of survival in a competitive world.

While her father floundered in his unwelcome status as widower, Tracy focused on easing his grief. Once he discovered the young widow, their lives diverged. The widow, Tracy had always suspected, posted herself in her father's presence by design rather than accident. Blonde, tan, and half his age, with three small children, she was a regular at his tennis club. Shortly after their marriage, he bought a rambling house in Westport, Connecticut for his new family.

Tracy knew she was always welcome there on weekends, but her pressing graduate school assignments became legitimate excuses for staying away from that socially active, youthful household. Pleased that her father was so enamored of his new bride that he seemed to have sloughed off a few years, Tracy was relieved that he no longer felt obligated to hover over her life like an unwelcome storm.

Instead, she turned to her advisor, Dr. Wendell Findlay, and his wife Nelly, a cheerfully plump woman, the antithesis of Mrs. Reynolds. Their cozy apartment was appointed with photographs taken during their journeys abroad to archaeological sites and bookcases stacked with professional journals, the classics, and volumes on world cultures. Tracy was mystified by the abundance of diverse religious materials scattered throughout the apartment until Nelly expressed her fervent belief in the power of prayer, no matter its cultural roots, and the responsibility of each individual to help his fellow man.

"The more Wendell tells me about ancient civilizations, the easier it is to see that their rise and fall was predictable," Nelly said. "Each civilization climbs to its peak because of people helping those around them to build a strong society. The end comes when powerful leaders are so consumed with acquiring riches and asserting their authority that their morals collapse. It's the same with individuals. The people we truly admire aren't those who gain fame by making money, but those who do the most for their fellow man." Nelly patted Tracy on the knee. "I'll stop philosophizing if you'll tell me about your young man."

"My young man?"

"You mentioned earlier that you were seeing someone who works on Wall Street."

"There's really nothing to tell you about Ken. He's an old friend. My mother liked him very much. I'm sure she would have been pleased if we planned to marry, but that isn't in the cards."

"No? Then you aren't committed?"

Tracy smiled. "Not at all. We do have similar tastes, such as relaxing in the country or at the theater, but it ends there. Our careers are as far apart as they can get."

Nelly smiled back. "It *is* a long distance from Lower Manhattan to Morningside Heights."

"The gap is even greater when I remember that he works in a plush office with deep leather chairs and executive bathroom privileges while I sit in a straight wooden chair in a cubicle overlooking Harlem."

"Wendell tells me that you thrive in that environment." Nelly leaned over and lowered her voice. "I shouldn't tip my hand, but I happen to know that he regards you as the sharpest T.A. in the department. There's a solid future for you at the university if you're willing to hang in there. It takes years to climb those ivy vines. Sometimes young women become discouraged."

"Never! I love what I'm doing and I certainly don't plan to let Ken or any other man keep me from finding out how far I'm capable of going in my career."

Those words haunted Tracy each time she and Ken went out on a date. Try as she may, she could not share his enthusiasm for a growing list of stock clients. He, in turn, suppressed yawns when Tracy brought up the subject of Chinese dynasties.

Something had to give. She never expected it to be her comfortable niche at the university.

The teaching assistant position paid very little, but the cramped carrel in the corner of an office shared by four faculty members was her private island, an oasis where she pored over student essays, devoured reports by archaeologists in the field, and idly wished she had the courage to embark on an adventure of her own.

The catalyst arrived unexpectedly in the guise of a flyer the department secretary tacked on the hallway bulletin board.

Tracy edged closer. The column headed "Opportunities" seldom listed anything that interested her, but this one captured her imagination:

Dr. James Baxter, Chairman, Anthropology Department, Eastern Arizona University, seeks assistant. Position begins in September. On-site summer training in archaeological methods required. All expenses covered by a grant.

Tracy gulped. The assistant's salary quoted was five times what she received as a T.A.

Even though her knowledge of archaeological methods was limited to what she had gleaned from books, she felt certain the on-site training could supply everything she lacked in that area. The grant meant that her bank account would remain intact throughout the summer.

Best of all, Dr. James Baxter was *the* authority on Southwest archaeology with a gilded reputation for scholarship and enough publications in recognized journals to fill a bookcase.

Tracy had never run across such a generous offer in the field. While the flyer did not specify the duties of Dr. Baxter's assistant, she read volumes into it, including future faculty and research openings.

If she ever wanted to make a career move, this was a way to leapfrog over Eastern university protocol. At the bottom of the T.A. pool with no promise of advancement over the long queue of Ph.D. hopefuls ahead of her, she was ready to pad her resumé by making a fresh start.

She jotted down the details. By the time she snuggled under the covers that evening, she had mentally composed a letter to Dr. Baxter outlining her background and assuring him of her ability to comply with his expectations.

The next step was to obtain a recommendation from her department head.

She hurried to Dr. Findlay's office first thing in the morning, then stopped abruptly in the doorway. He was deep in conversation with a tall, bearded man, typical of the many visiting academics who frequently sought out the esteemed anthropologist.

Tracy was about to slip away quietly when Dr. Findlay glanced up and peered at her over the rim of his glasses. "Come in, come in, Miss Reynolds. We've just finished."

To his guest, he explained, "This is Tracy Reynolds, one of my prize pupils. Now she's our department's most dependable T.A."

"Nice to meet you," the man said. He spoke rather brusquely, Tracy thought.

Before Dr. Findlay could complete the introduction, the visitor turned away from her and shook the older man's hand. "Thanks for everything, sir. We'll be in touch."

Ignoring the breech of etiquette, Dr. Findlay waved him away with a smile and confided in Tracy, "A fine chap. Sort of a relative on my wife's side. Now what can I do for you?"

He listened thoughtfully, his chin resting on his hand, while Tracy explained her reason for being there.

"Sounds like a wise move on your part," he said when she finished. "It so happens I'm on fairly good terms with Jim Baxter. He bent my ear at the symposium in Chicago last December about the archaeological field school he runs each summer on the San Marcos Reservation."

"Do you suppose that's where the training will take place?"

"More than likely. I understand that he draws graduate students from major universities everywhere. They pay top tuition dollar for the privilege of attending his field school, but the wording of the flyer suggests that the person chosen as his assistant doesn't pay a cent."

Tracy nodded. "That's how I read it."

"Then go for it full steam ahead." He paused. "Just keep your distance."

"What do you mean?"

Dr. Findlay chuckled. "Jim's reputation as a philanderer is nearly as famous as his reputation as a scholar."

Tracy blushed, even though Dr. Findlay was approaching retirement age and was as innocuous a gentleman as she had ever known. "I wasn't aware …"

He laughed out loud. "Have no fear. I hear he has a new wife. Must be at least his third, maybe his fourth. Anyway, his first love is archaeology, so you needn't be apprehensive."

"I can handle him on that score," Tracy said.

"That's the impression I get. If nothing else, you'll have a nice change of pace from the city in what I understand is one of the most remote and beautiful areas of Arizona. Glad to write a recommendation for you."

As easy as that.

Chapter 2

Tracy sent off the application. Then she waited.

Three weeks later, Dr. Baxter responded. The position was hers. There was merely the matter of completing a form waiving the right to sue the university for any injury occurring during the summer.

"That goes with the territory," her father assured her. "Forget about the unlikely dangers and just enjoy yourself."

Tracy was not surprised by his casual remark. He had become uncharacteristically laid back after his marriage to the widow, no longer the concerned parental figure she knew before her mother's death.

Once her plans were in place, she rang Ken.

"Hey, what's new?" The background office music, as usual, was intrusive.

"I'm quitting my job at the university and going to Arizona."

"Sounds sudden. Any reason?"

"It's an opportunity to do some hands-on archaeology and work with an expert in the field."

"You sure you're making the right decision? Arizona's a long way from New York. Once you're stuck in the boonies, it won't be easy to come back to civilization."

"It's not that isolated. After spending the summer on a reservation, I'll be working in town at the university."

"Knowing you, you'll cope. At the very least, it should be an adventure. If you decide the West isn't your cup of tea, New York will welcome you back. Look, Tracy, there's a call waiting on another line. I can't talk any longer right now, but let's plan to get together before you leave. How about Saturday?"

"I'd like that."

Seeing Ken that last time cleared the slate. If ever Tracy had expected something more serious to develop between them, those thoughts were laid to rest. She could not recall the movie they saw, only that it was pleasant with some humorous moments. Afterward, they stopped by their favorite shop for a hamburger and milk shake and held hands during the walk home from the subway stop.

The goodnight kiss clinched her decision. Swift and perfunctory, it was a kiss between two friends. Tracy read nothing into it except Ken's wish for her success in whatever project captured her fancy. Squeezing his hand with finality, she turned her attention to the rest of her life.

Several miles about the earth, Tracy glimpsed the alien landscape below and recalled Dr. Findlay's prediction, "You're headed for an experience you'll never forget!"

As the plane landed at Phoenix and taxied up to the gate, Tracy gasped at the unexpected palm trees and crimson sun hanging low over purple mountains. Both were foreign to her natural habitat.

Over the chatter bubbling from all sides, the flight attendant cautioned everyone to remain seated until the engines stopped. Once the doors opened, the passengers surged forward. Tracy clutched her bag with an intensity born of Manhattan living, half expecting a thief to grab it, but as she deplaned and entered the terminal, the friendly faces awaiting friends and relatives on board raised her spirits.

Relief washed over her. This is a place where life is relaxed, she thought. Everyone seems to be so glad they're arriving I know that Dr. Findlay was right. This opportunity to spend the summer on an Arizona Indian Reservation couldn't be topped.

Outside the terminal, she hailed a taxi. The lights of the city danced a welcome along the street to the White Mountain Bus Depot. There she would catch the next bus to Globe. Her trunk, shipped a week earlier, would be waiting there at the Dominion Hotel, along with the rest of the group assembled for the journey to Juniper Junction, the field school on the San Marcos Reservation.

The depot door opened automatically, coached by the electric eye that beamed Tracy's presence, but as she stepped into the waiting room, she halted abruptly. The line of travelers wound around the room twice in quest of two agents patiently trying to dispense tickets.

Never had Tracy felt so foreign in her native land. Most of the prospective passengers were Native Americans, as anthropologists termed them. Not for several decades would "Indian," the mistaken identity supplied by Christopher Columbus, fade from general usage. Others appeared to be itinerant cowhands. All males were roughly attired in jeans, boots, shirt, and cowboy hat. The women seemed newly arrived from another century in their long, colorful squaw dresses.

Tracy heard no voices, only the rhythmic thump of a stamp against an ink pad and jingling coins, followed by shuffling feet as those grasping tickets retreated to vacant seats among the rows of benches.

At length, she reached the counter and withdrew a bill from her wallet. "A one-way ticket to Globe, please."

The agent accepted her money, stamped a ticket, and shoved it toward her with the change. "That'll be tomorrow at noon, ma'am," he said.

"Noon! I have to be there before then. I intended to arrive this evening."

"Sorry. We make only four trips to Globe daily and they run full. The last bus pulled out three hours ago. Some of these people missed it and are waiting for the first one tomorrow morning at seven."

Tracy bit her lip, annoyed that the agent surveyed her with amusement at such a critical moment. Her suit, straight off the rack from Bloomingdale's, was not at home on the range. Good tailored clothes were a habit she had picked up from shopping with her mother, who worshiped the philosophy that it is far wiser to buy one smart outfit than ten sleazy ones.

The longer the agent stared at her, the more Tracy felt as if she were the one from another age, another planet. It was clear that the suit must be buried in the bottom of her suitcase at the earliest opportunity and replaced by reliable jeans and a cotton shirt. By now, all dark eyes in the waiting room were focused on her.

If her appearance caused such attention in a city bus station, she was bound to lure an unwelcome audience in the tiny desert town where she was headed. At that moment, she yearned to melt into the crowd.

She was about to turn away when the agent thawed. "Look, ma'am. If you can get up with the sun, I'll guarantee you a seat on the seven o'clock bus. It pulls into Globe by eleven."

"I'll be here," Tracy said swiftly, then hesitated. "The only problem is …"

"You don't want to sit here all night, so you'll need a place to stay," he supplied. "The Adams Hotel just around the corner on Central Avenue is a nice place."

Tracy wondered if she could believe him. One person's idea of a nice hotel is another's ruined vacation, her father always said.

"That's the truth, ma'am," he said. "One of the finest in the West. Been here for years, but it's up to the minute. Just one thing: they close the gates at nine and it's past that now." Touched by Tracy's visible dismay, he added, "Now don't you worry. When you ring the bell, the porter will open up for you."

"They actually lock up the hotel at nine o'clock?"

He laughed easily. "Lots of Easterners wonder about that. It's an old Spanish custom. Maybe there'd be less trouble other places if all businesses closed up early."

"You could be right," Tracy said. She thanked him for the ticket and the recommendation, picked up her suitcase, then hurried past the line of travelers. She had never dreamed that her first impression of Native Americans would be of their dogged stoicism in the face of interminably long lines at city bus stations.

The ticket agent had not exaggerated. Despite its sleek facade, the Adams Hotel reeked of Old World charm. Heeding the agent's advice, Tracy rang the bell. The wrought iron gates parted at once, ushering her into a spacious lobby rich in Spanish tile, warmly polished woods, and Moorish chandeliers. As he slid the room key across the counter, the clerk assured her that he would leave word for an early call.

"So you're going to Globe?" he pressed.

"Actually, I'm going beyond Globe," Tracy said, not wishing to divulge her mission to someone who seemed more than mildly interested. "I'm meeting some people there at noon. That's why I have to catch the early bus."

"I see." He waited for her to elaborate.

She smiled, closing the subject. She picked up the key, and walked to the elevator. Inside the cage, she jabbed the button for the fifth floor where her room was located, but before the doors closed, a man entered. Wary of being alone with a stranger, Tracy ignored him—until he doffed an enormous western hat and spoke.

"Pardon me, ma'am. I couldn't help overhearing you and the desk clerk. I'm heading for Globe early tomorrow morning, too. I'll be glad to give you a lift if you don't mind traveling in a truck instead of the bus."

Tracy regarded him icily. So this was how men operated in these wide open spaces! In his late twenties or early thirties, the stranger was uncommonly tall, of the rugged bearing unequivocally linked with the adjective "Texan." His manner was polite enough and his features were clean cut, even handsome, but his eyes—black as the shock of dark hair tumbling over his forehead—were so deep that she could not plumb the meaning behind his offer.

The prudence that comes to the fore after a lifetime in a teeming city supported her initial reaction. She responded as coolly and firmly as she could without revealing her fear at being approached by a stranger from whom she could neither flee nor hide.

"Thank you very much, but I've already got my ticket. Besides, I'm meeting some friends."

She tacked on that last white lie to suggest that concerned companions awaiting her at a designated place would report her missing if he dared to attack.

He was about to say something more, but at that instant the elevator halted at the fifth floor and the door parted. Her eyes averted, Tracy swept past him, relieved to emerge unscathed from the encounter. Only as she was unlocking the door to her room did she realize that he had exited from the elevator directly behind her and was about to enter a room across the hall.

Alarmed, she rushed inside, slammed the door, and activated the safety lock. Her heart continued to pound, even after she chided herself for harboring an unfounded fear of a mere traveler like herself. Still, she could not dismiss the possibility that the stranger played a role in a mysterious plot. Joining him on stage was not an option.

Chapter 3

Tracy slept fitfully. Perhaps it was the excitement of starting a new phase of her life. Perhaps it was her fear of missing the bus to Globe. Or perhaps it was determination to avoid further contact with the tall stranger across the hall.

When the sun filtered through the drapes shortly after five, she dressed, gathered her belongings, and quit the room, closing the door as quietly as possible. Rather than risk a chance encounter, she crept down an emergency staircase at the end of the hallway.

If the morning desk clerk was curious as to why Tracy entered the lobby from the fire exit, breathless and impatient to pay her bill, he expressed only the establishment's hope that she had enjoyed her stay and would return at her earliest convenience. Mumbling her thanks, she bolted for the bus depot.

The sheer number of patient Native Americans waiting there troubled her once again. A few sat on benches hunkered down for a long stay; most, however, stood mutely in line hoping to find space on buses already parked at the gate or on those expected momentarily.

Hungry and tired from too little sleep, she mounted a stool at the lunch counter. After contenting herself with a mug of rich coffee and a doughnut—a surprisingly flaky one, at that—she awaited the first bus to Globe.

Tracy was relieved to see that a large number of the patient travelers found seats on board. The driver, his bus filled to capacity, left the depot precisely on time and steered it purposefully through the city's palm-canopied avenues, past adobe residences painted in a rainbow of pastels, and onto a highway that served few travelers save the bus and occasional trucks. Toward the end of the first hour, he pulled up to a roadside depot, a combination gas station and lunchroom.

Tracy smiled to herself as she contemplated a forlorn sign: "*Apache Junction, Established 1953, Population 700 and Growing.*" As far as she could see, there was little nearby to tempt new residents unless they did not mind setting up camp among the few trailers scattered across the barren desert. Two Native American men leaving the bus were replaced by a woman and a small child. Silently, the newcomers passed down the aisle, eyes averted, and settled into the vacated seats near the rear.

Shortly after the bus pulled away from the dusty depot and turned onto a narrow country road, the vista changed abruptly. Ahead were the Superstition Mountains and scenery Tracy had admired hundreds of times in photographs, paintings, and on the silver screen. She knew now that landscapes she once believed were too rocky, too purple, and too photogenic to be real were not exaggerated. Formidable ridges loomed above the desert like castles guarding an alien planet.

The stark grandeur of the scene made her mindful of those whose ancestors adapted their lives to cohabit with nature. Now their descendants were beholden to the ways of powerful men.

Every so often, the bus slowed for a Native American waiting quietly by the roadside, perhaps a wizened old man seemingly stooped from the weight of his cowboy hat, or a young woman lugging a huge wicker basket. Occasionally, when the driver stopped for a passenger to board, another rider would disembark. Each acknowledged the other with a silent nod, a symbolic recognition of their ancient brotherhood, before proceeding on their separate ways.

Tracy marveled at the incongruity of the modern bus trespassing across the unspoiled pre-historic land. Beneath the shadows of the jagged pastel spires thrusting upward from the earth's crust, she felt humble and insignificant, in awe of the people who had survived in this fortress of plateau and canyon for thousands of years.

Throughout most of the journey, the highway followed a broad, flat course between mountains hovering at a respectable distance, but the sight of copper smelters belching great puffs of smoke heralded the road's descent into a gully slotted between low hills.

Just as the passenger agent had promised, the bus reached the outskirts of Globe within four hours, allowing Tracy more than enough time to rendezvous with the Juniper Junction group. From her seat, she viewed the town's business quarter directly ahead, an elongated main street comprised of shops and saloons lining a wooden walkway. It reminded her of early mining towns she had viewed in yellowed photographs.

The bus halted before a cafe, its official stop. Climbing down onto the sidewalk, Tracy saw her destination close at hand. The Dominion Hotel, directly across the street and the largest building in sight, was also one of the least inviting.

Smiling ruefully, she considered its façade. Frumpy at best and highly suspect at worst, it was hardly the sort of place a single girl alone in a strange town would choose, but she had no alternative. The mimeographed sheet mailed from Dr. Baxter's office had clearly instructed the recipient to forward all luggage to that address.

Crossing the street, Tracy mounted the wooden steps past a Native American squatting in the shade. The veranda, though rickety, was sufficiently substantial to support a row of dilapidated rocking chairs playing host to several elderly men, their rheumy gazes fixed upon the opposite hillside. Once through the creaking door into the lobby, Tracy paused several moments while her eyes adjusted to the gloom.

Lazy ceiling fans battled the relentless heat. An elderly woman guest on a faded mohair sofa fanned herself with a magazine. The desk clerk, wrinkled and brittle, could have been there since the hotel opened a century earlier. He listened politely as Tracy explained her mission.

"I need to pick up my trunk now so I'll be ready to leave for Juniper Junction at noon," she concluded.

The man scratched his head, pondering the situation. "Well now, I don't remember a trunk coming for someone named Tracy Reynolds, but that doesn't say it didn't. Another young lady from your group checked in last night. Hers ain't here neither."

Tracy winced at the thought of surviving the summer in the single pair of jeans and shirt her suitcase held. "You don't suppose it's lost, do you?"

"Hard to say," the clerk drawled. "Sometimes things show up ... sometimes they don't."

"Could you check, please? I need to know if I'll have to run out and buy more clothes." Tracy was shocked by his slow, easy reaction to what loomed as a major disaster. The cost of replacing her clothes, sleeping bag, blankets, and the heavy boots she had shipped in the trunk would take every penny in her wallet.

The clerk shuffled from one foot to another. "Why don't you go up and see your friends while I look out in the shed?"

"My friends? Is the group from the university already here?"

"I don't think the big guy they call Doc's here yet. He comes every summer, so I'd recognize him for sure. Just those two girls showed up last night. They're from the East, like yourself."

Tracy glanced down at her tailored suit, by now slightly rumpled, but nevertheless a sure giveaway in these hills, she told herself. The sooner she changed into the native costume, the better she could melt into her surroundings. Aloud, she said, "I'll do just that … if you'll tell me their room number, please."

"Sure thing. Next floor up. Just take those stairs over yonder. Turn to the left. Third room on your right."

So saying, he limped through a swinging door behind the desk, presumably on his way to the shed. Tracy picked up her suitcase and headed to the stairs.

She climbed the narrow passageway paved with carpeting worn through to the bare wooden stair treads beneath. At the landing, the stale heat mingled with cigarette smoke embedded in the faded wallpaper. Tracy felt little remorse for not having made it this far the previous night.

Her knock was greeted by the sound of scuffling feet and muffled giggles. She was about to rap a second time when she heard someone fumbling with a bolt on the other side. As the knob turned from within, the door cracked open. She stared into an eye level with her own.

Chapter 4

Tracy returned the gaze. "Are you with the group going to Juniper Junction?"

With that, the door swung wide, the eye settling into its normal territory, a broad, friendly face. "I was afraid you were one of the bunch we heard whooping it up all night at the saloon across the street," said the girl belonging to the eye. "Come on in."

"Thanks. I'm Tracy Reynolds."

"And I'm Iris Meyers from Boston College, about to switch from anthropology to romance languages if this kind of place is our destiny." Rolling her eyes, she ran her fingers through limp, stringy hair desperate for a shampoo. "You'll think I'm lying when I tell you that I was queen of my high school senior prom. This is about as grubby as I've ever felt, and with no hot water on tap in this joint, someone's bound to mistake me for yesterday's leftovers. So what brings you to the end of the world?"

"I've been teaching basic courses at Columbia, but I'll be working at East Arizona starting this fall."

"Becky's from Bryn Mawr, no less. You'd never guess from her appearance that we're in snooty, Philadelphia Main Line company."

Iris pointed to her companion crouched on the bed. A rumpled shirt, soiled jeans, bare feet—toenails caked with dirt, and pierced ears studded with safety pins clashed with the sweet face framed by braids about to unravel.

"Hi there," Becky said with a chuckle that accepted Iris's description in the spirit intended. "At least I'm better dressed for the job. When are you planning to get out of those duds?"

Tracy laughed out loud. "Right now, if you don't mind. It's lucky I brought a set of work clothes along because the desk clerk thinks my trunk hasn't come."

"That's exactly what happened to Becky," Iris said, guiding Tracy toward the bathroom. "She says she doesn't care, but some of the rest of us might—if we have to live with her very long."

"Picky, picky, picky," Becky crooned from the bedroom as she fiddled with the radio dials. That phase of civilization's march had not been lost to Globe, Tracy observed.

"At least yonder left-over hippie has a pleasant disposition," Iris said, *sotto voce*. "We met on the train out of Chicago. Kept staring at each other until we finally decided we must be headed to the same place. After two days in a passenger car with cinders flying through the open window and one night in this flea bag, I have to admit that she's the sort you can put up with in lousy situations. Daffy, but bearable. Now look at this, would you?"

Iris indicated the fixtures with overly dramatic gestures. "A bathtub with legs, one of them missing and replaced with a wooden block that wobbles. And a water closet fit for a museum."

She demonstrated by pulling the long metal chain. Water streamed from a vat positioned near the ceiling. Tracy roared, unable to help herself.

Iris shook her head. "Admit it. We must be crazy to spend a summer in a place like this. And we're still in town, if you can call it that. Go ahead and get changed so we'll be ready at the witching hour. If you hurry, maybe we can get out of here and be gone before anyone finds us."

She closed the door, leaving Tracy to replace her travel outfit with the less conspicuous jeans and shirt.

The minute she stowed the suit in her bag and kicked off her heels, Tracy felt better. The sneakers imparted such an enthusiastic bounce that she forgot about her lack of sleep. The longer she sat and chatted with Iris and Becky, the better she felt about everything. The missing trunk slipped her mind entirely until Iris consulted her watch.

"Up and at 'em," Iris said. "We're due in the lobby right now."

Already they had agreed that none of them knew what to expect of the summer. Becky confessed that she was hoping to immerse herself in pottery. Iris said she would be content to pick Dr. Baxter's brains. Tracy said little. She hoped she would pass muster as his assistant—on a strictly professional basis. Relieved to close the door of the cramped, antiquated room behind them, the trio headed down the staircase to meet their companions journeying to Juniper Junction.

Upon entering the lobby, Tracy stopped short. She was not prepared for the imposing figure striding toward them.

Dr. James Baxter was a western film hero, not a fiftyish bone hunter. His sideburns and the dark hair framing his forehead were tipped with silver, but the icy blue eyes peered from a tanned, unlined face that towered above a frame worthy of inclusion in a physical fitness advertisement. He doffed a stylish western hat and extended a hand to each of them in turn.

"Well, well! You must be our ladies from the mysterious East. I'm Doc, and you are …?" "Iris Meyers."

"Becky Whelan."

"Tracy Reynolds."

Doc's powerful handshake and penetrating eyes rendered them speechless. Tracy felt her cheeks flame as Doc assessed her from head to foot. "Ah yes, Tracy. Dr. Findlay and my spies say you're ideal for the job, and I can't agree more. How do you like Arizona so far?"

"Fine. Just fine, Dr. Baxter."

"That's 'Doc' to you, and to everyone, for that matter," he said. "Promise me there'll be no more 'Dr. Baxter.' Everyone at Juniper Junction is on a first name basis. We're all one big family up there. That's why it's such a special place. He turned to Iris. "Now then, what are you going to call me?"

"Doc," she replied.

Already she was breathless, reduced to mush, and when Doc laughed, hugged her, and said, "That's right, Iris," she turned a brilliant cerise.

Tracy sensed that Doc was savoring their reaction as an ego builder, if nothing else. He beckoned to some others seated on the mohair divans. At his signal, they rose and ambled over. All wore friendly smiles, Tracy noticed, except for the striking redhead in the vanguard who conveyed to all by the manner in which she commandeered Doc's arm that she had a claim on him.

"These are the rest of our group, Julia," he told the redhead. To the three young women, he said, "This is my wife, Julia, who insists on keeping tabs on me by coming to Juniper Junction, even though she prefers dressing up to getting down to earth in the dirt. Right, darling?"

"Your students know that you're always right," Julia laughed. Her voice, cool and dusky, lacked emotion. Tracy could not tell if she was being serious or sarcastic.

"Well then," Doc boomed. "It looks as if we're ready to roll."

Tracy spoke up. "Not quite."

"Something wrong?"

"My trunk. The desk clerk says it hasn't come. I have to check back with him."

"Uh-oh. The same old problem. Nobody ever allows enough time for delivery. But don't worry. Snakeskin will look into the matter."

"Snakeskin?"

Doc summoned a young man with a thick beard and twinkling eyes. "This is Snakeskin Somerville, our resident ethnologist. Snakeskin, this lovely lady is Tracy Reynolds."

"Howdy," Snakeskin said, offering Tracy a large, rough hand. She liked him immediately.

"He's not such a rube when he's lecturing to the students," Doc said. "In fact, he and Greg are the brains behind this entire operation. I just come along for decoration. Greg's going on ahead to open up camp with Clarence, our cook. That means huge problems like fair damsels losing their trunks fall into your hands, Snakeskin. Think you're up to it?"

"Easy," Snakeskin grinned. "Why don't you all head for the trucks and I'll try to bail you out, Tracy."

Becky piped up, "While you're at it, see if mine has come."

"Sure 'nuff." Snakeskin drew a rumpled paper and pen from his breast pocket and jotted down the details as Becky repeated them. "The railroad agent holds the trunks until the spirit moves him to haul a load to the hotel. Guess the spirit's tendin' to someone else's problems."

Leaving Snakeskin behind, Tracy and the others followed Doc to the street. Already a caravan of trucks and station wagons lined the curb.

"Here's our gang," Doc said. "You'll meet them all later, that's for sure. I always like to put the gals and guys from the East in with the folks who've been to Juniper Junction before. You'll get to know some people on the way and they'll give you tips on survival in the wilderness."

True to his promise, Doc separated Tracy, Becky, and Iris. Tracy learned that her driver was Ray Garrett, an osteologist, or bone specialist, on the staff at State. At his side was Marie, a graduate student. Tracy climbed into the back with Rosa, a dark, quiet girl from Texas, and Brenda from Colorado. Heavyset and shy, Brenda said she had just graduated from State and hoped to get a job with the university museum in the fall.

Rosa explained that she had a position as high school history teacher lined up for the fall in her home town, El Paso. After pursuing a career in anthropology for more years than she dared to admit, she was drawn to a public school job and the steady salary it offered. The summer at Juniper Junction would be her final fling with like-minded friends before facing an unknown classroom. At the very least she would use her experiences there to entertain reluctant students.

During their brief exchanges, Tracy found them all so pleasant and open that she felt she had known them for years. While they awaited the stroke of twelve, the scheduled departure time, Doc traveled up and down the sidewalk conferring with the drivers to make certain their vehicles were stocked with ample fuel, water, and emergency supplies should they become separated from the caravan. Just as Tracy was about to resign herself to a single change of clothing, Snakeskin appeared around the corner wheeling her trunk.

"You're in luck, Tracy," he said. "They're up to their old tricks again. Nobody at the station bothers to deliver the trunks to the hotel until they're good and ready. They figure that folks who want their things bad enough will come after them. I was pretty sure I'd find your trunk because this happens to at least one person every summer."

A surge of relief swept over Tracy. "You've saved me, Snakeskin. Thanks ever so much. But what about Becky?"

Snakeskin shook his head. "That's another story, I'm afraid. She'll have to do with what she has for two weeks when I come back to town for supplies."

Marie gasped. "Can you imagine going two weeks without a change of clothing? I hope she's not assigned to my cabin."

"I knew this would be a summer full of laughs," Brenda said.

"You can't mean that," Rosa said. "Especially with Greg hanging over us."

Brenda nodded in agreement. "You are so right. He's the fly in the ointment I could do without."

Tracy's ears perked up. "Who's Greg?"

Brenda made a face. "Greg Delgado, the geologist. "You'll meet him soon enough. Doc won't do anything without him. It's been that way every summer I've spent at Juniper Junction. Greg graduated from State several years ago, then went to work with an oil company, but he keeps coming back like a bad penny. I guess this is a vacation for him, but it's not one for us when he's around."

Tracy frowned. "He's tough to work with?"

"The worst! He's a perfectionist," Rosa said. "No matter how hard you work, he always puts you down."

Ray glanced back at Tracy through the rear-view mirror, his eyes twinkling. "The ladies resent Greg because he insists that they do their work properly," he said. "He keeps them slaving so hard they don't have time to goof off."

"Oh, you!" Marie slapped his arm playfully. "Greg puts everyone through their paces all right, but that's not the only thing." She peered hastily in all directions before continuing in a low, secretive tone. "There's something odd about him."

Ray sighed. "She doesn't mean that, Tracy."

"I do, too." Marie was adamant. "It's very strange that Doc refuses to do anything without Greg's approval. You'd think he was the boss and Doc was the employee."

"That's not so strange," Ray said. "Doc was Greg's advisor in school and they've been good friends ever since. He's older and more experienced than most of us at camp, so Doc relies on his judgment."

Brenda drew herself up. "Don't make excuses for him, Ray. Marie is exactly right. There's something very strange about the way Doc lets Greg handle most of the field work. He directs the dig, heads up the lab, and even grades our lab notes!"

"You sound like old hands at Juniper Junction," Tracy said. "I thought coming here would be a once in a lifetime opportunity for most people."

"Maybe for someone from the East, but those of us at State know this is the only way for an anthropology major to spend the summer," Ray said. "No two digs are alike. There's always new information to learn, new sites to uncover, new strains of pottery to discover …"

"And new romances," Marie said, not waiting for him to finish. "Ray and I got together by sharing a common grave site. He did the muscle work, I whisk-broomed the burial, and the result was out of this world. We didn't have much chance to be alone on the job, though. Greg gave us lots of grief if we so much as crumbled a tiny piece of skull bone. He may know what he's doing, but he's much too serious. I don't understand why Doc tolerates him. He's anything but a cheerful addition to the camp. If I didn't know that Doc is one of the world's greatest lovers of the ladies, I'd think there's something weird between them."

"Come on, Marie," Brenda said. "There's no danger of that. No, if you ask me, I think that Greg has something on Doc, sort of a threat he hangs over him."

"It struck me that way once, but they're too chummy for that," Rosa said. "Personally, I don't care what's going on in their lives. I just don't like answering to Greg for my work when Doc's the one in charge. As long as Greg keeps his distance, I'm happy."

"What you mean is that you want to be free to pursue Doc," Marie said, laughing.

"Me and ten others," Rosa said.

Brenda turned to Tracy. "Don't let their talk fool you. Doc likes the ladies, but Julia makes him toe the line. She's his umpteenth wife—well, maybe his fourth. They've been married three years now, and I haven't heard a bit of scandal about him in that time except for wishful thinking from every female student in the department. Still, there's always room for hope, at least that's what I hear. Say, speak of the devil. There's Greg!"

Tracy followed Brenda's gaze. At first, she saw only a dusty truck pulling alongside, the driver saluting Doc to signal his departure. As suddenly as he passed, a chill ran through Tracy, defying the blazing heat. Her view, though brief, was vivid enough to reveal Brenda's "devil" as none other than the man in the elevator.

Chapter 5

Tracy had dismissed all thoughts of her elevator companion the moment the bus pulled out of Phoenix, assuring herself that the encounter had been harmless, not sinister. She even conceded that she would manage a shade more civility if they met once more. But after hearing her new companions voice their suspicions about Greg, she concluded that her first impression had been right on the mark.

No matter what Doc thought about him, the exchanges she had heard offered concrete reasons to keep Greg at a distance. She was mulling over ways she might remain aloof throughout the summer when Ray cut into her thoughts.

"Where's your hat, Tracy? You'll die of heat prostration the first day without one."

"I brought a scarf," she said. "That should be ample protection."

Brenda frowned. "Don't kid yourself, Tracy. If you don't have one of these, you'd better hop out right now and pick up one at that supply store across the street."

Reaching behind her seat, Brenda drew out a tattered straw hat. Its brim, sloping fore and aft, curled about the ears.

"Brenda's right," Rosa cautioned. "You won't last an hour without a hat. Out here, it's your best friend. I'll help you pick one out. Come on."

Tracy and Rosa climbed out of the station wagon and crossed the dusty street. Several Native Americans huddled near the store entrance. An elderly cowhand leaning against the a streetlamp stared at the young women dispassionately.

Rosa drew open the screen door and ushered Tracy into a room aromatic with tobacco, leather, straw, and denim. The counters and ceiling-to-floor shelves held wares of every description. Deep barrels were stuffed chest high. What could not be accommodated elsewhere hung from the rafters.

"Here's what you want." Rosa pointed to a stack of round-brimmed hats.

"I'd rather have one like yours, with a rolled brim," Tracy said.

Rosa smiled. "This is how they start. You have to add the personality."

Tracy selected one, then tried in vain to roll the stiff brim. "It won't budge," she said. "Are you sure yours was like this when you bought it?"

"They all are," Rosa said. "Water does the trick. Let me show you."

After Tracy paid for the hat, the clerk directed them to a sink where Rosa demonstrated how to soften the brim by soaking the straw.

"Now keep rolling and holding the sides in place while they're damp," Rosa said. "By the time the hat dries, the shape is permanent."

As the hat began to assume the cocky air she desired, Tracy glanced into the mirror to assess her appearance. "It's big enough, that's for sure," she said. "If this doesn't keep off the sun, nothing will."

"Sun and rain both," Rosa said. "By rolling up the sides, you've made a trough so the water can run off at either the front or the back. You'll stay a lot drier than you would if it poured onto your shoulders."

"Pretty ingenious. But there won't be much rain to worry about here, will there?"

"You never know," Rosa said. "The rainy season that locals call the monsoon period comes in late July. Thunderstorms like you've never seen! By then, you'll be so baked by the heat that you'll welcome every bolt of lightning."

"You talk as if you've seen plenty of rain at Juniper Junction."

Rosa nodded. "Enough to be as awed by the weather as the natives are. The lightning sparks forest fires that can get out of hand and surround you, if you're not careful. That's why Doc always gives us fire-fighting training the first week of camp. If the rangers call on us to help out, we'll know what to do."

She gave Tracy's hat an approving nod. "That's coming along well. Keep holding the sides in place. The straw'll dry in a hurry while we ride in the heat. It's a little bit like setting your hair. Come on, now. Let's get back so they don't go without us."

They reached the station wagon just as Doc stuck his head in the window to tell Ray that everyone else was accounted for. "We're ready to roll, folks," he said. Seeing Tracy wearing her hat, he smiled and winked. "Now you look like a full-fledged Westerner, Tracy. Very becoming."

Tracy blushed, swept into the stream nourished by Doc's charm. Marie marked Tracy's reaction. Once Doc was out of ear-shot, she said, "It never fails. That famous Doc Baxter smile can turn a straight-laced women into a puddle of jelly." Before Tracy had time to protest, she added, "You'll get over it when you meet some of the other guys at camp. Off hand, I'd say that you're Bill Harrison's type. Don't you think so, Ray?"

Ray grimaced as he switched on the engine. "Don't be so eager to pair everyone up, Marie. Tracy seems to have a mind of her own."

"I'm sure she does, but I'll bet anything she likes Bill. He's so good looking." Marie rolled her eyes.

Ray tossed her a grin. "If you find him that attractive, how come you didn't go after him instead of me?"

"That's easy. I like security. Besides, I'm rather fond of you." Marie gave Ray a playful hug to prove her point.

As the caravan pulled away from the curb and steered down Globe's main street, a clock began striking the hour and a fire whistle moaned. High noon.

Chapter 6

"We'll reach camp in plenty of time for supper," Brenda said.

Marie groaned. "Don't even mention food. I'm hungry already thinking about Clarence's heavenly meals."

While Marie rambled on about the delights awaiting them at Juniper Junction, Tracy listened politely, her eyes drinking in the alien landscape beneath a sky checkered with wispy jet trails. They had traveled some distance along the highway when she saw Doc's truck, at the head of the caravan, turning onto a narrow gravel road. One by one, the other vehicles followed his, their tires agitating waves of dust.

As far as Tracy could see, gaunt clumps of grass vied with the elements for survival amid sparse growth that Ray identified as mesquite and Joshua trees. Once Tracy saw a road-runner scurry under the welcome lobe of a prickly pear, hesitating in its shade until the convoy passed. Further along, Ray pointed out a coyote flattened by a passing vehicle, tire tracks imprinted upon his back.

With each swirl of dust through the windows, Tracy sucked in her breath. Conversation ebbed as mouths remained sealed against the grit. The stillness was sliced only by the thrum of the engine and loose stones peppering the sides of the station wagon. Ray switched on the windshield wipers to worry the dust trying to coat the glass. When Tracy tried to glimpse the trucks following behind, she could not see beyond the dense clouds churning in their wake.

"Don't worry, we can't lose each other," Ray said, marking her concern through the rear-view mirror. "We simply follow the dust of those up ahead. This is the worst leg of the trip. We're almost to the San Marcos Trading Post. When we leave there, we head for higher elevation. It's not so dusty once we reach the grasslands."

By the time they pulled up to a cluster of wooden buildings, Tracy saw that Doc was already out of his truck and peering under the hood to check the radiator. Slamming it shut with visible satisfaction, he opened the door on the passenger side to retrieve Julia. She took his arm before stepping onto the ground. Distaste for the dust was reflected in her face as she tiptoed alongside Doc toward the trading post.

"We might as well hop out and stretch," Marie suggested.

"I need something to drink," Rosa said. "Anyone else coming in?"

"I'll join you," Tracy said, climbing out of the station wagon.

Inside the trading post, they bought cold drinks and exchanged greetings with the others. When Iris and Becky dragged in, Tracy could not help laughing.

Iris groaned. "Don't say it. I don't need to be reminded that I passed up a summer on the Cape for death by dust bowl."

"Ooooh, look!" Becky's cry lured Tracy to a case filled with silver and turquoise jewelry. "It's better than a museum!"

At that moment, Doc appeared beside them. "Do you like it?"

"It's fabulous!" Tracy said. "Is it made right here on the reservation?"

"The contemporary pieces are. The older ones could have been with local families for several generations." He directed their attention to a corner case fortified with padlocks. "These come from much earlier times. Look at that silver work. It's cruder than the newer pieces. Since it was done long before techniques were streamlined, the imperfections are easy for a layman to see. Instead of taking away from the value, they make it far more desirable." He paused until he had Tracy's full attention. "If we're lucky, we'll find examples this summer that go back even earlier."

Tracy frowned. "We'll dig up jewelry like this? I had no idea ..."

Doc laughed. "It's not likely, but we can always hope. Most of our sites go back long before the early inhabitants had enough leisure time to make fancy jewelry. There's always the chance, though, that we'll find something from the transition period when the simple bone adornments were replaced by crude silver and turquoise pieces."

Iris wanted to ask more about the jewelry, but Doc waved her off. "Later, Iris. We'll talk about this another day. Right now, we'd better get started or we'll never make camp by supper."

Doc nodded toward the man behind the counter. "Frank says Greg passed through nearly an hour ago. That means we're falling behind. If you thought we were going slowly over the road this far, wait until you see what's coming.

Frank says a washout this spring tore up the trail, but we can make it if we take it easy."

One by one, they filed out of the trading post. Just before Tracy reached the door, she heard a whispered exchange behind her. Glancing back, she saw Frank shove a small parcel toward Doc. In return, Doc placed a wad of bills in the Apache's hand, then turned his attention to Julia, who stood at the end of the counter, a worried expression on her face. There was no time for Tracy to wonder about the contents of the package. Once outside, she heard Ray start the engine and saw Marie beckon her to hurry along.

After pulling away from the trading post, the vehicles proceeded along the gravel road for several miles until it converged with a narrow dirt track. A weathered sign up ahead pointed to Fort Beacon. Ray explained that it had been an Army outpost before Arizona was a territory. Now it was merely a small Indian settlement more than fifty miles distant. Abruptly, Doc turned onto the narrow track, the others close behind. Soon they began to climb.

It was an easy grade at first over slopes broken by occasional mesquites, squatty barrel cactus, and yuccas, but as the path wound through broken rock cliffs, the engine of Ray's station wagon strained, sputtering ominously, until they breasted a ridge that quickly gave way to thick groves of juniper and piñon pine, ultimately to a flat track bordered by tall grasses.

More than an hour had elapsed when the caravan entered a narrow gap between hills and slowed to a crawl. "Thank goodness ...," Tracy began, believing they had reached their destination.

Brenda laughed. "Don't get your hopes up. Doc always stops here for a drink."

Peering toward the front of the caravan, Tracy saw a stream plummeting down the hillside and across the road. As if on signal, the trucks stopped. Everyone spilled out and followed Doc to the water. There Tracy learned a valuable use for her new hat by watching the others quaff the cold liquid as quickly as they scooped it up.

Their thirst quenched, the drivers checked their radiators and replenished water bags. Once all travelers were refreshed, Doc hustled them back into the vehicles, the engines were fired, and the convoy forded the stream, navigating without incident through deep water lapping at their underbellies. After mounting a narrow trail up and over the bank, they proceeded along a forest track.

Some time later, they burst onto a vast plain, beyond it a seemingly endless horizon. Tracy marveled at the sweeping panorama that continued as far as the eye could see to tall mountains, several capped with snow. Between the trail they traveled and the distant wooded hills, acres of unbroken pasture land were dotted with cattle.

"It looks like a huge ranch," Tracy said.

"That's exactly what it is," Rosa said. "The tribe raises cattle here."

"It's their main livelihood," Ray said. "Sometimes they drive their herds through Juniper Junction on their way to Fort Beacon."

Marie tossed Tracy a warning glance. "Just be careful they don't catch you digging up one of their ancestors."

Tracy snapped to attention. "I wondered about that. Do they resent the university operating on their land?"

"Not to our faces, but I wouldn't be surprised if the tribal leaders take a stand some day to let us know that we're not welcome," Ray said. "A lot of them regard archaeologists as invaders of sacred land. They may be right. Say!" Changing the subject, he pointed to a distant wisp of smoke. "Look over there!"

Rosa clapped her hands. "At last! We're coming to the Apache settlement."

"It won't be long now," Marie promised. "Their village is only three miles from Juniper Junction."

Several dozen wickiups were clustered beneath tall pines. As the caravan approached, Tracy saw women sitting before looms positioned on the shady side of the buildings, their colorful skirts echoing the colors of the brightly patterned rugs they wove. Children played nearby.

"The women don't seem very interested in us," Tracy said.

"You wouldn't think so, but they're really ever so excited," Rosa said. "They don't exhibit curiosity the way the kids do because they've learned to be passive. They know that the people who work at Juniper Junction are friendly and not like the white men they've dealt with in the past. I suppose that's why they tolerate us here, even though it goes against their beliefs for outsiders to disturb their burials."

"If they're like other native societies, they probably think our presence here brings bad luck," Tracy said.

Ray nodded. "They *know* it's bad luck, but they also know that we're the ones who'll be punished in the end. They just watch ... and wait."

Tracy glanced around at the others. "Do you agree with them?"

"After you've been here a summer, you'll believe anything," Marie said.

Once past the settlement, Tracy leaned forward in her seat, straining to see through the dust-streaked windows. Her first view of Juniper Junction was of low, rustic cabins scattered through the trees. Directly ahead, a water tower was bounded on either side by large, substantial buildings. Marie identified one as the dining hall and kitchen, another as the infirmary, and the largest as the combination classroom, laboratory, and Doc's office. Further beyond, another group of cabins and several small structures were arranged haphazardly beneath the trees. In the distance, a vast plain stretched toward the horizon.

Ray pulled into a parking area alongside the classroom and cut the engine. "Welcome to Juniper Junction, one and all."

Everyone tumbled from the vehicles, eager to shake off the dust and grime. Conversations ceased when Doc motioned for silence while he assigned the cabins.

"Cabin One … Cabin Two …," he called, systematically reeling off the names of their occupants until Tracy heard, "Cabin Seven, Tracy Reynolds …"

The list completed, Doc announced that supper was scheduled to begin in one half-hour at the sound of a gong.

Marking concern on Tracy's face, Rosa whispered, "Don't worry. We have enough time. It's easy once you learn the routine."

Tracy shot her a look of mock helplessness as she strained to move the trunk Snakeskin had unloaded onto the ground. Just as she was beginning to make headway, a voice at her side said, "I'll get that."

She whirled around to see who had spoken, masking her emotions with the stern, practiced expression that repelled unwanted attention. To maintain an outward appearance of composure, she stifled the gasp that fought to surface. Throughout the drive, she had known he would be at Juniper Junction. Even so, it was a shock to once again gaze into the face of the man in the elevator.

Chapter 7

"Didn't you hear me? I said I'll take your trunk." Greg towered above her, an enigmatic smile on his lips.

"There's no need," Tracy lied.

"Don't be silly. You can't manage by yourself." Ignoring her feeble protest, Greg hoisted the unwieldy thing onto a cart and dusted off his hands.

Tracy hesitated, not quite willing to admit defeat.

"Well come along," he urged. "It's nearly suppertime and there's a lot to do."

He began wheeling the cart across the grounds. She followed, several paces behind. Before they had gone any distance, he paused and waited until she caught up. "We were both headed in the same direction after all," he said.

"So it seems." She hoped he understood that her cool response was a blanket refusal to become involved in his murky doings, whatever they were.

Tracy deduced that he received her message loud and clear because he said nothing more before resuming his task. She lagged behind deliberately. By the time she reached the cabin door, Greg had parked her trunk in the middle of the floor and was on his way to assist someone else, without so much as a curt adjournment.

"That's old Greg. A real cool customer."

The relaxed voice was coming from the far corner of the cabin. As Tracy's eyes adjusted to the shadows, she could see a young woman stretched out on a cot. "I'm Diane Freeman," the voice said, in response to the unspoken question.

Before Tracy could introduce herself, Diane continued, "When you've been here as often as I have, doll, you'll learn to high-tail it fast to your cabin before the rest arrive. This is my favorite. It's away from the others, so there's lots more privacy, and this is the best cot because it's not next to the window. Keeps me warm on cold nights. I hope you don't object."

"I guess you've earned it," Tracy said. "I don't mind the cold, not after today's heat."

"When the early morning temperature drops to freezing, you'll change your mind," Diane promised. As Snakeskin wheeled in two more trunks, she added, "Well, look here. Our cabin mates have arrived."

"It's Brenda and Iris," Tracy said. "We've already met."

"Doc likes to mix the old-timers with the greenies," Diane said. "Brenda and I can help you two. To begin, you can toss your bedding on the cots and your clothes on these shelves."

"I see you've taken the most convenient ones," Iris said.

"That's one of the lessons you learn here," Diane said.

The newcomers unpacked swiftly, then followed Brenda to the pump for water. By the time they toted the brimming pails back to a rickety stand outside the cabin, the gong was sounding. Tracy paused only long enough to scrub her hands and splash her face before falling in behind the three other occupants of Cabin Seven. With Diane in the lead, they sprinted to the dining hall where the others were already vying for seats at the long tables.

The meal was beyond Tracy's hungriest expectations. Roast beef—right off the range, Doc pointed out—was fork-tender. There were huge bowls of mashed potatoes, tureens of savory gravy, platters of freshly picked corn and tomatoes from the garden Clarence had been tending since spring, and aromatic breads, both white and whole wheat, straight from the oven. For dessert, there was a chocolate fudge cake on every table and bottomless jugs of coffee, the best Tracy ever tasted.

Between mouthfuls, Brenda turned to her and said, "The food alone is worth the trip. Clarence is a culinary genius. During the school year, he cooks for the football team, so he's an expert at preparing in quantity. Like the athletes, you don't have to worry about stuffing yourself because you'll work it all off on the dig."

Tracy felt her weariness drift away as she consumed her fill and listened to the animated conversations all around the table. Voices reached a loud crescendo before Doc rose and rapped on his coffee mug.

After formally welcoming everyone to Juniper Junction, he presented those seated with him at the head table. Julia, his wife, had sat quietly throughout the meal, her head bowed over her plate as if she were intent on locating the least fattening morsels. Upon hearing her name, she looked up, wiggled a bejeweled hand in the air, and manufactured a smile that faded as quickly as it came. Tracy could not decide if Julia's aloofness was caused by shyness, boredom or petulance.

Next, Doc clapped his hand on the shoulder of Greg Delgado seated to his other side. "Greg's my right-hand man. As always, he'll be in charge of the lab, the sites, and every other aspect of camp life in the event I'm not available."

Greg rose and smiled tentatively amid faint, scattered applause. Tracy conceded that his imposing presence matched Doc's at first glance, but the sea of glum faces in the dining hall suggested that something was amiss. It was clear to her that the animosity Greg generated among those who had tangled with him in the past was as strong as their outpouring of affection for Doc.

Why, she wondered, would Doc delegate authority to someone who was so obviously unpopular and secretive?

Snakeskin Somerville, seated next to Greg, oozed all the personality and boyish charm Greg lacked. After taking a few minutes to outline the field trips and recreational activities he had planned, he sat down to appreciative cheers.

"Snakeskin is such a great guy," Marie whispered to Tracy.

Tracy nodded. "It's easy to see that everyone likes him."

Continuing with the introductions, Doc presented Dr. Stanwood Morgan and his wife Shirley, the camp nurse. "We're lucky to have such a top-notch medical team, but they'll be forever grateful if everyone here keeps out of harm's way," he said.

"Call me Woody," the doctor said, as he rose and waved. "You folks know that we snap up the chance to work on the dig every summer. I need the privacy and mental housecleaning after a putting in an academic year at the university hospital, and Shirley's rock hound nose gets to follow the scent to ancient treasures. The worst that can happen is a snake bite or a broken leg if someone falls off the pueblo. I hope you'll respect my privacy and not bother me if you're the victim."

Everyone laughed politely. Woody looked so casual to Tracy that she found it hard to believe he would have enough presence of mind to fabricate a cast for a broken bone. In any other setting, his unkempt appearance—shirt unbuttoned far enough to reveal a thick mat of chest hair—might cause a casual observer to mistake him for a social misfit. That was further proof, she reminded herself, that appearances can be deceiving.

As Woody sat down, Doc motioned Clarence out of the kitchen. "This is the most important member of the staff. Let's have a round of applause for Clarence and his crew, Jerry, Mack, and Ed. They just graduated from Tucson High

School, so this is their introduction to the real academic world. Maybe they'll get their fill of it this summer and decide to ship out with the Navy instead of enrolling at the university in September."

The four left their tasks long enough for a group bow to hearty applause, then returned to the kitchen.

The staff out of the way, Doc asked the rest present to rise one at a time and introduce themselves. Tracy learned that she, Iris, and Becky were the only ones from the East. The others came from universities west of the Rockies, the majority of them seasoned visitors to Juniper Junction.

In addition to those Tracy had met already, there were Bill Harrison, highly recommended by Marie, and four young men whose jeans, shirts, and cowboy boots were tinged with an expensive aura peculiar to those who work hard at wearing a casual air.

R. J. Bradley, Tracy noted, bore his brash good looks with a clean sophistication that dovetails neatly with money. Stu Billings and Joe Lawson, less striking in appearance, seemed to be cut from the same cloth as R. J. The upper crust glow even managed to shine through the carrot top and sea of freckles belonging to Red Vernon.

Tracy knew that her assessment was valid when Diane leaned over and whispered, "Those are the Psi Theta boys. Always together. They room in Cabin Three. Been here for the past two summers courtesy of dads with bottomless bank accounts. They're nice enough guys, but they'll never have to work for a living. They hang out here for the fun of it. Must want to see how the other half lives."

Marie overheard. "On the other hand, maybe they want field experience while they're young so they can enjoy the prestige of chairing a department in their middle age without having to worry about living off a professor's salary."

"University pay is far better today than it was a few years ago," Tracy said. She was pleased with the salary East Arizona promised her come the start of the fall semester, although she admitted to herself that any amount of money would have made her happy if it came with hands-on experience at Juniper Junction and the chance to work under a mentor of international reputation like Doc.

"No matter, you still have to work an angle to survive," Iris said. "I've known lots of professors who rely on the joy of being independently wealthy like that good looking quartet over there." Wistfully, she added, "I wonder if they like Eastern gals."

"But what about Doc?" Tracy countered. "He's famous in his field, and yet he's devoted to research and teaching. Surely he doesn't have time to make money on the side."

"Maybe not, but he and Julia live on an ultra-plush ranch outside of Willcox," Diane said. "And just look at her clothes! They're not off the rack, so either she has a whopping inheritance, or he has a gimmick."

At that moment, Tracy heard Doc call her name. As she stood to acknowledge the introduction, she caught a better glimpse of Bill Harrison. He was every bit as handsome as Marie had promised. She sensed his eyes riveted on her, as well, and as they filed out of the dining hall for a brief lecture in the lab, she saw him coming her way. He caught up with her just as she stepped onto the porch.

"First time here?" he asked.

"You probably could have answered that without asking," Tracy said.

"Actually, I could, but I couldn't think of a fancy way to pick you up," he said, his eyes twinkling. "Where you come from, the guys must have a sophisticated line."

She smiled back at him. "Yours is as good as any."

As they moved into the building, he told her that he had just finished a graduate degree in business, but anthropology was his hobby. "This is the third summer I've spent at Juniper Junction. It'll probably my last because I need a job." Grinning, he added, "It looks as if this will be the best summer ever."

Tracy thought it best to remain silent. She moved to follow Brenda into the first row of chairs, but Bill clutched her arm and steered her to a corner seat. Across the room, Marie made faces to attract Tracy's attention. "I told you so," she mouthed.

Flattered though she was, Tracy turned her attention to Doc, who was requesting silence from his perch on a stool at the front of the room. After briefly summarizing the Southwest cultures, he reviewed the method of recording finds in the field by a grid system. Those familiar with the system doodled while the newcomers took copious notes.

"This system allows curators and researchers years from now to pinpoint exactly where each item was found," he said.

Tracy took notes so frantically that the detailed instructions soon became a jumble in her mind. She expelled a heavy sigh.

Bill leaned over and patted her shoulder. "Don't worry. It sounds impossible when you're sitting here, but once you're out on the dig, everything makes sense."

"Thanks for the encouragement," she whispered. "I hope you're right."

As they emerged from the lecture room, Tracy saw that twilight had replaced the vast red sunset. Electric lights strung through the trees outlined pine needle boulevards between the buildings.

Before the group broke up, Doc conducted them on a quick tour of the camp to point out the bath house with separate showers for the men and women and a washing machine.

Iris perked up "No dryers?"

Doc gave her a withering look. "We use fresh air here. For your convenience, there are yards of clothesline strung between the trees."

The camp's rustic flavor extended to the rather grand outhouses, set at opposite sides of the camp, one for each sex.

"These are the Green Kivas," Doc said. "I'm sure all you newcomers know that the name is derived from the pueblo houses of worship."

"Absolute sacrilege," muttered Becky, the purist.

Doc laughed. "There's plenty of that here to go around. Now it's time for everyone to sleep. You've had a long day and the gong sounds at six. Breakfast is fifteen minutes later. If you miss it, you'll get mighty hungry before the next meal. The truck leaves for the dig sites by seven. Late-comers have to walk."

"He means business, but everyone loves it," Brenda said. "They suffer just to please him and to uncover a patch of history never before known to modern man."

Bill came up behind them. "Don't believe her. It's not all hard work here. There's plenty of time for fun, if you know where to find it." He took a firm grip on Tracy's arm. "Come on. I'll walk you ladies to your cabin so I can learn my way there in the dark. The lights go off at ten, you know, and it's black as pitch here after that."

Tracy frowned. She had come to Juniper Junction to work and learn, not to become romantically involved.

Chapter 8

Diane had not exaggerated about the cold nights at Juniper Junction. Snuggled in her sleeping bag, weighted beneath a thick blanket, Tracy woke intermittently, shivering. When the morning gong sounded, her nose felt like the proverbial icicle.

She groped sleepily along the unfamiliar shelves to locate her warmest clothes, then dressed in haste before tackling the high boots worn to guard against snakes and rough stones. Once they were laced properly, she went outside to scoop a bowlful of icy water from the buckets. Out of the corner of her eye, she saw some of the others stumbling along the pathway to and from the Green Kiva. Many were rubbing eyes still caked with the sandy remnants of sleep.

To Tracy's surprise, everyone managed to assemble in the dining room on time, their voices coming to life as tall jugs of steaming black coffee made the rounds. When the ham steaks and heaping stacks of hot cakes had passed from the head of each table and back again, all were ready to tackle the world.

Canteen slung over her shoulder, straw hat in hand, Tracy joined the group assembled several hundred yards from the camp on a rise overlooking the plain. Doc and Greg stood apart, speaking earnestly in low voices, while the others chatted among themselves. The rails of the stake truck parked nearby were lined with the picks and shovels Doc had promised.

Tracy inhaled deeply, mentally composing the letter she would write to Ken. Even though he had been a city dweller all his life, he had enjoyed their many weekend drives through the countryside. For a brief moment, she wished he were with her to share the view.

The morning sun, voluptuously rimming the peaks to the east, had already banished much of the chill. Beads of dew still clung to tall tendrils of prairie grass. Hawks soared and swooped against the sky, a vivid blue backdrop to the cottony clouds scudding gleefully before the incessant wind.

With a clap of his hand, Doc ended Tracy's reverie. "All right now, when you old-timers are excused from this exercise, you can grab your tools and head for your assigned locations, but the newcomers aren't going anywhere without a lesson in handling the tools and eye training." He assumed the pose that Tracy already recognized as his way of demanding undivided attention from his audience. "A lot of you know that I can sense projectile points wherever I go. Isn't that right, Greg?"

Greg, unsmiling, nodded in assent while Doc deliberately covered his eyes and turned himself around several times. "Now! Let me see if I can find one lying right ... about ... here!"

So saying, Doc plucked a perfect specimen from the dust and held it aloft. Tracy heard several gasps expelled nearby. Doc chuckled, pleased with himself. "It's simply a matter of training. By the time the summer ends, you all will be finding projectile points wherever you walk. Isn't that right, Snakeskin?"

Snakeskin, chewing on a stalk of grass, nodded affably.

For the next few minutes, Doc explained their assignments, the excavation of two separate sites. The first was an early Mogollon village. "Greg, Snakeskin, and I scouted it last summer. We call it Forestdale."

Becky giggled. "It sounds like a suburban housing development."

Tracy saw Doc raise an eyebrow. At that moment, she understood that the egotist in him needed to be surrounded by "yes" men and have the floor at all times. Snakeskin played his role well. Greg was another matter. Even though he agreed audibly with Doc whenever addressed, she had seen him clench his jaw more than once, as if deliberately biting off something he wanted to say. Tracy remembered the comments made by Marie and Brenda. More than ever, she was beginning to believe Greg capable of sinister actions if given the opportunity.

Although Becky's remark had been innocuous, it drew attention away from Doc. He waited, pointedly, until the tittering ceased and all eyes were once again on him. "The only drawback to Forestville is its location in woods filled with rattlers," he said. "That means I'm looking for the bravest crew possible."

With a volley of shouts, most of the men bounded into the bed of the truck. Tracy cringed involuntarily at the mention of snakes, yet the aspect of danger seemed to be the very spark needed to lure volunteers.

"See you later, cutie," Bill whispered in Tracy's ear.

Deliberately ignoring the "I told you so" expression Marie tossed her way, Tracy turned in the opposite direction and saw Greg watching her with a quizzical expression on his face. He looked away the moment their eyes met.

Once the Forestville crew piled onto the truck, Red Vernon studied the map Doc handed him, then slid behind the wheel and steered onto the dirt track. Tracy lost sight of them even before Doc beckoned those remaining to gather close.

"Everyone on my right will be working on strat tests—that's short for stratigraphy," he said. "You'll be looking for potential sites to excavate further, so pick a friendly partner." Then he turned to his left, facing Tracy. "You folks will begin on the broadside of the pueblo we started to excavate last summer"

As they moved toward a second truck pulling alongside, Iris turned to Tracy. "What on earth is a broadside?"

Rosa overheard. "It's a ton of dirt that turns into a sore back, stiff joints and a throbbing sunburn."

The teams clambered into the back of the truck, while Doc swung into the cab, sandwiched between Greg at the wheel and Snakeskin.

"Hang on!" someone shouted, and the truck began to move down the bumpy track, spinning stones in its wake, until it reached the level plain. There it veered from the trail and struck out across the grass. After a mile, it stopped to discharge the first team, followed by several others at regular intervals. At each stop, Snakeskin helped the team set up their equipment before jogging off to meet the truck at the next stop.

As the truck pulled up to the pueblo site, Tracy caught her breath. Each of the rectangular rooms was perfectly outlined and separated from its neighbors by thick stone walls. Despite harsh winters, the arid climate had prevented erosion and preserved the pueblo exactly as was hundreds of years earlier. Now it lacked only a roof, the residents, and their primitive artifacts.

"It's like an apartment complex," Tracy said.

"There's no community pool or playground, but the view is spectacular," Rosa said.

"Except for that huge pile of dirt," Iris said.

Tracy glanced in the direction of the far wall. "I'll bet that's where we begin."

Her suspicions were confirmed when Doc clapped his hands for attention. "All right. There are six rooms across, one for each of you. The top layer of the broadside has piled up over the past five or six centuries. Beneath it, you should find a trash pile. We can tell a lot about people from their garbage."

"One man's trash is someone else's treasure," Becky said.

This time, Doc laughed at her remark. "That's right, Becky, and we're the treasure hunters. After the first pueblo dwellers left, people from the south moved in and built their homes on top of the original structure. They threw their trash over the side, and that's what we're after. Your first task, though, is learn how to dig with the right technique."

While Doc talked, Greg fetched the tools from the truck and handed everyone a shovel. At the broadside, Doc demonstrated how to scoop a shovelful of dirt and fling it off to the side with a flip of the wrist. It looked easy to Tracy, but when she tried, the dirt blew into her face. To make matters worse, Greg strode up and down the broadside, shaking his head. Even Rosa, Diane, and Marie, despite their past experience, were unable to please him.

At the sight of Becky's eyes filming with tears, Tracy understood why the others resented Greg. She was preparing a snappy comeback to his sarcasm when he stopped before her and said, "Looks like you're getting the idea, Tracy. Let your wrist do more of the work, and keep those shoulders still. Very nice for the first time."

She was so astounded and secretly pleased by Greg's assessment of her progress that she could not react until he was gone. By the time he drove back to the site to collect everyone for lunch, Tracy was beginning to feel like a professional ditch digger, handing out pointers to Becky and Iris, and ignoring Diane's warning to pace herself.

"You'll be so stiff you won't be able to get up tomorrow morning," Diane cautioned. "Take your time. The dirt's been here for centuries. It won't go away."

Tracy rode back to camp in the bed of the truck prepared to pounce on whatever Clarence had prepared for lunch. She was not disappointed. Hamburgers, huge cauldrons of baked beans, and a crisp salad were topped off by giant brownies, enough left over to stuff in knapsacks for afternoon snacks on the site.

By the end of the working day, the hot shower and fresh clothes were even more welcome than the batter-fried chicken and hot apple pie, but the day's strain told on Tracy before the evening lecture ended. Afterward, everyone gathered in a circle beneath the pines to sing along while Snakeskin strummed his guitar. In other circumstances, Tracy's voice would have competed with the loudest of them. This time, it faltered as she fought to keep her eyes open.

She was not even aware that Bill had slipped down beside her until she heard him say, "How about a walk around the camp?"

"Thanks anyway, but I'm about to drop off. This routine and the altitude need some getting used to. Let me take a rain check."

"You can believe I'll take you up on that. At least let me walk you back to the cabin."

"Why not?" Tracy wobbled as she rose.

Quitting the camp site, they cut across the road and through the pines, chatting casually about the day's work. At the cabin, Tracy said goodnight and was about to enter when Bill shifted gears abruptly, positioning himself between her and the door.

"Excuse me …," she began.

"Surely the lady won't deny me a kiss for escorting her home," Bill said. He leaned forward, but instead of allowing him to put his arms around her, she ducked beneath them and scooted through the door. "Sorry," she said from behind the screen, "that's not included in the rain check."

Sheepishly, Bill stared at her for a fraction of a second, then turned on his heels.

Tracy smiled to herself. She was about to secure the door when she saw someone slip from behind the trees and follow Bill. She could not identify the pursuer in the dark, only that it was a man intent on remaining anonymous.

Chapter 9

Early the following morning, Tracy's team attacked the broadside. Once Doc was satisfied they could proceed without him, he left to monitor the team working at Forestdale.

About mid-morning, Greg came by. His facial expression and the notebook he carried told Tracy that he meant business. After poking through the backfill and retrieving bits of bone, chipped stones, and chunks of charcoal, he beckoned everyone to his side.

"You're throwing away good evidence," he said. "Some of these bones tell us what kinds of game the people ate. Others have been carved into jewelry."

Iris considered the bone fragment Greg was turning over in his hand. "That doesn't look like much to me."

"If you were observant, you'd see that this piece matches another one you've discarded." So saying, Greg reached into the dirt and produced a small curved segment of bone. It fit precisely with the other.

Iris frowned. "What does that tell us?"

"These are sections of a bracelet. You might find the other missing piece nearby. If not, the owner probably threw these out because it was broken and no longer useful."

Tracy understood. "So we're looking for clues in the garbage dump about the lifestyle of the people who lived here."

Greg nodded. "We can tell a lot about a civilization by its utensils, the way people decorated themselves, and the food they ate. If you throw out vital clues, you destroy our chance of understanding the chain of events that led from the earlier civilization to this one. How many of you are recording every item you find?"

Each team member stood motionless in the heat. Tracy shared the guilt that accompanies undue haste as Greg scanned each notebook in turn. As he closed the last one, he sighed. "If you don't do it right, there's no sense in doing anything. This is a research project, not a beach party."

This last was directed to Rosa, who had removed her shirt to reveal a halter top beneath. She lavished suntan lotion on her shoulders as he spoke.

Marie stuck out her chin. "You don't have to be so critical, Greg."

"That's my job," Greg snapped. "Your mistakes reflect on Doc and the credibility of this project."

He wheeled about and left as abruptly as he had come. Tracy watched him take enormous strides across the prairie until he seemed to shrink in size, too small and distant to be a threat. She was about to return to her task when she noticed a figure on horseback emerge from a distant stand of pines.

The rider galloped at a rapid clip parallel to the broadside. Tracy concluded that it was an Apache cowboy working with a nearby herd, so she was surprised when he suddenly shifted direction, moving this time toward Greg. As if responding to a shout, Greg stopped. Turning toward the oncoming rider, he raised his arm in recognition and waited. Momentarily, the rider pulled alongside Greg and dismounted. Tracy wished she could overhear their conversation, but they were safely out of earshot. She resumed digging with one eye on the two men.

"Greg hasn't changed a bit," Diane said. She gave no indication that she had seen the distant exchange. Her next words convinced Tracy that she was merely brooding over his remarks. "He's the only bad apple in the lot, just itching to take his nasty disposition out on everyone."

Tracy startled herself by rushing to his defense. "He does have a point."

Diane eyed her with suspicion. "Even so, he could be nicer. We don't claim to be experts."

"I guess our only defense is to take our time and account for every scrap we find," Tracy said.

Becky groaned. "At that rate, it'll take a lifetime to finish this section."

Marie picked up her shovel. "Who cares, if we get Greg off our backs!" She removed a layer of soil far smaller than those she wielded before he arrived.

Taking the cue from her, the others began working slower. Tracy wondered if their lethargy could be blamed on their reaction to Greg or the sun boring into their backs. At her next opportunity to glance in their direction, Greg and the rider were gone.

When the truck arrived to ferry them back to the camp for lunch, Tracy could not remember ever working so hard for such meager results. She flung herself up into the truck bed and squatted by the rails, too weary to stand.

Back in the dining room, she became aware of whispers going around about Greg's high-handed attitude. If he sensed the displeasure, he did not let on. Throughout the meal, he conferred with Doc in low tones and what Tracy was beginning to believe was his characteristic unsmiling manner.

Once the last crumbs of gingerbread disappeared from the communal platters, Doc rose. "I'm aware that there's a problem with some workers hurrying through the preliminary soil layers," he said.

Tracy noted that he repeated exactly what Greg had told them at the site, but he spoke in a jovial, encouraging manner with no trace of criticism. Even though she had begun to feel discouraged about her progress, Doc's pep talk renewed her enthusiasm. She vowed to unearth every grain of soil in a professional manner and weave the thread of history placed in her charge into an accurate tapestry.

That evening, she began a letter to Ken. She described her surroundings, comparing them with those she had known all her life, and wrote in detail about the varied personalities and how they interacted with one another. She was careful to keep her report upbeat and avoid saying anything that might cause him to believe she missed him, for, in truth, she did not. He was merely a good friend, a connection with the past that she did not wish to sever abruptly. There was so much to tell that it took her several evenings and a sheaf of notebook paper to give justice to the Juniper Junction community. After sealing the envelope, she jotted a note of thanks to Dr. Findlay for helping her secure her position, and added a few lines about the nearby Apache settlement and the native traditions that she thought would interest Nelly. When they were ready, she deposited both letters in the mail sack hanging in the dining room. Snakeskin would take it along and post the contents during his supply run to Globe.

The days that followed were marked by such close and personal encounters with the earth that Tracy could not distinguish her co-workers from coal miners as they trooped off to the showers each afternoon. At the end of two weeks, Snakeskin made his much awaited journey to Globe and picked up Becky's belated trunk. For the interim, Becky had made do with the clothes on her back and those others lent her. Free spirit that she was, she did not seem to mind the inconvenience.

At the post office, Snakeskin exchanged the mail bag for another filled with letters awaiting delivery to camp. Tracy received a hastily scribbled page from Ken saying that he was leaving for two weeks in France and alerting her to watch for a postcard he would mail her from Paris. He also made brief mention of a new comedy he had attended on Broadway, leaving her to surmise that he had not gone alone. The thought of his stepping out with another woman did not bother her in the least. Already their close ties were unraveling quite naturally, easing her fear of hurting his feelings.

Tracy's favorite part of the day was the evening lecture. She marveled at Doc's ability to infuse dry topics like corrugated bowls and dendrochronology with the glitz of a theatrical production. Still, she often wished that he would shorten his talks so she could transfer her field notes from the dusty, smeared pages onto fresh sheets of paper. Once each week, she handed them in to be graded, sometimes by Doc, more often by Snakeskin or—worse yet—Greg, who was ruthless with red slashes through entire paragraphs. He picked minutely at technical accounts, scale drawings, sketches, even handwriting.

"He must think he's the Great White Father," Iris muttered, as the broadside team labored in the lab late into the evening trying to edit hastily scrawled notes.

Diane grunted. "To Doc's mind, he's perfect. That's why he has a free hand in the lab and out in the field. He says he's trying to make the research look good, but I think Doc lets him handle the dirty work to avoid the responsibility of telling us we're doing poorly."

"I ignore Greg," Rosa said. "In the long run, Doc's the only one we have to answer to."

"Yeah, but Greg stays a little too close for comfort," Diane said. "Always seems to be looking for something."

"Maybe there's something sinister going on at Juniper Junction," Rosa mused. "Could be I'm joining mainstream society just in the nick of time. High school students have their problems, but nothing much more troublesome than acne and dateless Saturday nights."

"Hush now," Tracy said. "If you don't knock it off, I'll never get these measurements right." She bent over the table, trying to translate the meters of her broadside section into inches. At length, a shadow fell across her paper and a large hand reached over her shoulder.

"Here's your metric measure on the other side," Greg said, flipping the ruler over. "It's easier to work with scales that match."

Tracy's mouth flew open. He had been standing there all along, listening. If he was angered by the remarks, his face bore no expression other than the stern, set jaw that belonged to him perpetually.

"I ... I ... I never noticed."

Greg's eyebrows shot up. "A competent archaeologist notices everything." He left as quietly as he had come.

With the passing of another week, the broadside team leveled the dirt to a tough clay layer. Tracy had scraped clean her area except for one corner filled with soft black earth. She was about to remove the remaining fill when something gave her pause. Shading her eyes from the sun, she discerned an oblong outline.

"Becky! Iris! I think I've found a burial."

Because the grave was not long enough to hold a human being, she deduced that the rest of it was nestled beneath the high section of wall still standing. To uncover the entire burial, she must begin digging once more from the top.

The broadside team, glad for an excuse to stop working, ran to her side. At that moment, Doc was making his morning rounds. The wind carried their shrill voices in his direction. When he caught sight of six figures jumping up and down in celebration, he lost no time in reaching the broadside.

If Tracy had any doubt about the value of her discovery, there was no mistaking Doc's broad grin. He stood for a long time contemplating the profile of black earth, and when he finally spoke, it was as one professional to another.

"Ah yes, Tracy. Just as I suspected. Already the grave furniture is exposed."

Tracy saw that nothing escaped his trained eyes. What had appeared to her as a lump of clay was the rim of a jar protruding imperceptibly above the soil. Doc ran his hand over it lightly, closed his eyes, and spoke as if in a trance.

"You'll have to remove the wall, of course, before you uncover the grave. When you pull everything down to this level, the complete grave will be clearly outlined. I suspect you'll find more pottery. There might even be some important jewelry because I have the feeling that this is a rather distinguished member of the society. Go slowly. Sift every grain of earth. We'll want an exact record of your progress, so be sure to stop at each level for photographs." He smacked his lips. "Yes, it looks very good."

Tracy marked that Doc was reacting like a man who had suddenly been granted the gift of eternal life. She returned his smile and accepted the praise he lavished upon her.

"It's all yours, Tracy, but you'll have guidance all the way," he said. "If something comes up when I'm not around, Greg knows what to do."

By the day's end, word of Tracy's "find" ricocheted around camp with speed that would have shocked the owner of the bones that had waited a thousand years to be discovered. Tracy jumped off the truck, still feeling the afternoon's high, but instead of hitting solid turf, she found herself in Bill's arms. He seemed to materialize from out of nowhere, as fired by her success as if it were his own. Embarrassed, Tracy pushed him away, laughing all the while as she protested her appearance. She excused herself hastily and followed Iris and Brenda to the cabin to grab a change of clothing before heading to the shower.

That evening, Doc began his lecture by announcing Tracy's find, whetting appetites for comparable discoveries. Buoyed by all the attention, Tracy was so wide awake after the class that she accepted Bill's invitation to take a walk.

They strolled away from camp aimlessly. The moon, in its fullest stage, illuminated the countryside so splendidly that Tracy could distinguish individual stones on the ground, even needles on the pines lining the pathway. They chatted about their work until the sound of voices and glow of lanterns directly ahead intruded on their conversation.

Tracy was the first to notice. "It must be the Apache camp!"

"We couldn't have gone that far," Bill said. Hastily, he added, "Well, maybe we have, but let's not worry about them."

He moved closer until the moonlight on his face framed a flash of white teeth. Reaching out roughly, he pulled Tracy to him and kissed her with far more passion than their small talk had promised. Instinctively, she drew back, breaking free of his hold. Alarmed that he had misinterpreted the friendship she was willing to share, she tried to speak casually. "If my grave inspires you that much, I'd hate to think how you'd react to an entire burial ground."

"Try me." Just as he reached out to grab her once more, she swiveled in the opposite direction and began running back toward camp.

"I feel a sudden urge to exercise," she called over her shoulder.

Bill tried to catch up, but he was no match for Tracy. Her high school coaches had trained her well. She jogged rapidly and evasively to elude his reach. After several hundred yards, both settled down to a steady pace. By the time they rounded the final bend, the camp was dark. All had retired for the night except for one dark figure moving quietly behind the pines.

Someone headed for the Green Kiva, Tracy thought. "Good night," she called to Bill as she took the last stretch to her cabin, leaving him far down the gravel track.

The long walk and the unplanned run sapped every speck of energy Tracy felt earlier. She collapsed onto the cool pillow and slept without surfacing once to dream about the ghosts flitting across the plain and through the pines outside the cabin door.

Chapter 10

During his second supply trip to Globe, Snakeskin learned that the forest fire conditions were rated "Extreme." No rain had fallen since early spring, a clear warning that the dry tinder and grasses could ignite easily. Along with Ken's promised postcard to Tracy all the way from France—a photo of Paleolithic drawings in the cave of Lascaux—he brought word from the reservation's chief forest ranger that everyone at Juniper Junction must prepare for an emergency. Instead of working on her burial the next morning, Tracy attended a class in fire fighting. Even the cooks participated.

Tracy giggled to see Clarence clumping about the woods in heavy boots and a straw hat instead of his chef's cap, but his transformation was not nearly so pronounced as Julia's.

Her visibility thus far at camp was limited to mealtimes; the rest of the day, she busied herself with cheap novels, crossword puzzles, and the mystic rite of sun bathing. Trace scents of her lotions and perfumes lingered in the shower room that she utilized while the others groveled in the field.

On this occasion, Julia arrived clad in designer pants and a tailored shirt instead of her usual halter-top sun dresses or long, glamorous skirts. Her perfect hairdo was protected by a Stetson hat. Gingerly, she selected a shovel from the pile to avoid chipping her elaborate nails. Although she listened intently to the instructions, she tarried well behind the active line, managing just enough industry to maintain appearances.

From a distance, Tracy watched Greg set deliberate fires at calculated intervals. Once they sparked to his satisfaction, he signaled Doc and Snakeskin. The moment it became evident that the smoldering brush would soon flash into flames if not contained, they commanded everyone's attention. Successful management of the crisis depended upon how quickly and how well the group constructed fire lines. Tracy immediately grasped the seriousness of the situation. A few sparks could torch the entire mountain unless every cinder was stamped out. Along with the others, she applied all the strength she could muster to beat each outbreak into submission.

For three hours, they toiled against the silent, onrushing enemy. Tracy's nostrils burned and her body became limp from digging trenches, raking ashes, and passing heavy water buckets along the fire brigade. By the end of the morning, the teams had succeeded in containing the blaze. From Greg's initial pyres, it had rampaged to within a few feet of the nearest building. Only during the final minutes was their victory assured over the vicious licks of flame straining to feast upon the tall, dry grasses and stately conifers in anticipation of racing toward camp structures and consuming them.

Spent, her mouth cottony from thirst, Tracy dropped down on the ground alongside several others while Clarence and his crew prepared the belated lunch. The quiet conversations nearby confirmed that the practical lesson proved to be more dangerous than first anticipated. Doc's visible relief when Greg signaled a successful end to the exercise was not exaggeration; he had not expected the small fires to persist so stubbornly.

"I guess we were very lucky," Tracy remarked to Julia, who leaned against the adjacent tree, too tired to return to her cabin, yet too fastidious to slump down on the ground.

Julia's voice was low and bitter. "If Juniper Junction burned down tomorrow, it would be a blessing."

Tracy fumbled with a response. "I think it's a wonderfully exciting place." No sooner did she utter those stilted words than she knew they fell upon hostile ears.

"You'll change your mind when you know more about it," Julia said. She glanced around furtively to make certain they were not overheard. "People aren't always what they seem to be. I was trusting and naïve, like you, until I learned that everyone has a secret they'll do anything to hide."

Tracy took that as a warning to keep off forbidden territory and refrain from testing Doc's reputation as a lady's man. Disappointed that Julia could believe her capable of stepping across moral boundaries, she said, "I think most of us are here to work. I know I am."

"No, no, no," Julia said. "You don't understand. I'm not criticizing you, Tracy. I'm cautioning you to keep your eyes open. Don't be gullible. Be open to making a difference. When you're my age, you'll shrug your shoulders and try to ignore what doesn't concern you, especially if it hurts others. If it touches you, well, that's another matter."

Tracy forced a laugh. "I'm afraid you're talking over my head. Are you referring to our work, to the people here, or to the camp itself?"

"All of those ... and more. You and some others are new and couldn't possibly know, but if you keep your eyes open, everything should become clear."

Just as Tracy was about to reply, Julia's eyes warned her. Bill was approaching.

He greeted Julia perfunctorily before tapping Tracy's shoulder. "Lets head on up to the dining room. Maybe Clarence can give us some carrot sticks to munch on until the meal's ready."

The mention of food propelled Tracy to her feet. "Sounds good to me. Care to come along, Julia?"

Julia's mouth curved faintly. "Thanks for asking, but I'm going back to the cabin to change. You go ahead, but ... you won't forget what we talked about, will you, Tracy?" She placed a beautifully manicured hand on Tracy's sleeve. "It's important!"

Tracy studied Julia's eyes. No longer cool and secure, they registered naked fear that shuddered through the fingers gripping the younger woman's arm.

"Of course I'll remember. Can we talk about it another time?" Tracy tried to smile reassuringly. She felt genuinely sorry for the beautiful woman who no longer projected the impression she could handle any disaster, major or minor, with aplomb.

Tracy's response seemed to satisfy Julia. She dropped her hand, the cloak of self-assurance settling over her as swiftly as it had fled. "Yes, let's do." She tossed that over her shoulder so casually that she might have been confirming a luncheon date. She moved away, presumably to escape the heat and lingering smoke in order to freshen her make-up.

By the time lunch was over and the teams drove to the site for the afternoon shift, the schedule had been compromised. There was only enough time for Tracy to remove a surface layer and bag a few pieces of crumbled pottery. The next day, however, she accomplished much more, penetrating seams of rock and ash until she came upon a layer of charcoal speckled with charred bone, the remains of someone's roasted game.

She paused, wondering how many centuries had passed since unknown ancients cooked that meal. Who were they?

Had they ever contemplated the future?

Did they suspect that another human would one day search impersonally through the puzzle pieces they left behind?

The deeper she dug, the more she collected. Her sacks soon bulged with cracked earthenware, bits of bone, and tools made of obsidian, the hardened lava belched up by nearby volcanoes. Each time Doc visited her site, he seemed to be operating on a higher level of enthusiasm than before. When she showed him a jasper ornament and a perfectly preserved shell necklace, he clapped his hands together with the glee of a child at his birthday party.

By the time Tracy had filled seventeen bags of artifacts to be store in the laboratory until she could catalog them, Snakeskin arrived with his photographic equipment. He explained that he would film it twice, first before she opened the grave, later when she exposed the contents. She brushed excess soil from the face of the wall, as he directed, and waited for the sun to reach an optimum angle.

That moment arrived a few minutes past noon, shortly after Doc drove up. He extolled the photogenic aspects of the site, and even insisted that Tracy kneel alongside the grave in one picture. Snakeskin, ever cheerful and patient, shot from every angle Doc suggested. Once Doc was satisfied that the burial location was duly recorded for the museum files, he ordered Snakeskin to cover it with a tarpaulin for protection from the weather, inquisitive animals, and curiosity seekers. Even though it crossed her mind, Tracy did not have the courage to ask Doc if he expected repercussions from the nearby tribe.

The following morning, with Doc, Snakeskin, and her team gathered around, Tracy exposed the contents. First she uncovered the skull, beautifully preserved, then the undisturbed skeleton, and finally the grave furniture, two jars in mint condition.

Doc was elated. "Tracy, these are splendid specimens. A Tularosa fillet-rim bowl and a McDonald grooved jar. Exactly what I thought we'd find!"

"Did your theory hold up?"

"Theory?" Doc seemed to be caught off guard.

Tracy quoted from her notes that referred to the key point of his lectures. "The theory that Juniper Junction was producing art objects a thousand years before the New World was discovered, a lot earlier than previously believed."

She thought he seemed distracted as he replied, "Well, of course."

Half joking, Tracy said, "If you can date this grave as you hope, you'll have anthropologists in every university in the country squirming and trying to jump on your bandwagon."

Doc did not smile. When he spoke, his voice, ordinarily booming and jovial, was so soft that Tracy felt excluded from his presence. "I can! And I will! All my work is leading to one fact: the dates we've been working with are all off by a thousand years. I'm the first one to disagree with my colleagues. When I'm gone, they'll remember me for that, if nothing else. Everything written about these civilizations is the product of educated guesses. I'm here to change the books by digging down deeper than anyone else has gone."

Tracy watched a smug, uncharacteristic smile spill across his face. She had the fleeting impression that she was being used as a pawn. Deep down, she believed that most scholars and scientists would consider a reputation like his sufficient reward at the height of a career, and yet she could not shake the impression that Doc was driven by a craving for something missing in his life.

Even as she stared at him, trying to probe beneath his façade, he emerged from his trance as quickly as it had enveloped him. He dusted his hands. "Well, enough of this. Let's cover the grave for the night. Tomorrow we'll photograph it before it's dismantled for the lab. Then you'll have your work cut out, my dear."

The following morning, Snakeskin took the final shots in optimum sunlight from all angles should the museum curator one day wish to recreate the scene in a display case. Then Greg drove up with Ray, who examined each bone before Tracy transferred it to a container.

"Jot this down in your notes," Ray told Tracy, ticking off every fact his expert eyes could verify. "It's a male, about forty. He broke his left femur at fourteen years …"

Tracy interrupted him. "How do you know that?"

"Take a look. Right here is where the bone mended." Ray ran a dusty forefinger over a small bump. "He must have walked with a slight limp for the rest of his life because this bone is shorter than the identical one on the right leg. Now, lets see … ah!" He sat back on his heels and motioned to Doc. "Take a look at this node on the humerus."

Doc stroked his chin. "Tuberculosis of the bone. That's what did him in."

"Sure fits the pattern doesn't it, Doc?"

Tracy pressed Ray. "You've seen others like this?"

He nodded. "Hundreds. It's one of the most common causes of death in this area over a thousand year period, and it usually hit them by middle age. They didn't worry about our modern causes of death: heart attacks, cancer, strokes. They died too young to develop them. Things haven't changed much for the Native Americans in all these years. Tuberculosis is still a major killer."

"Then this burial isn't so unusual," Tracy said.

"Doc grabbed her by the shoulder. "Not so unusual! Tracy, darling, it's a prize! First of all look at the way he's laid out. Must have been a shaman or a leader of some kind because of the grave furniture. And the bowls are proof that the Tularosa and McDonald wares were made long before anyone suspected. Tell her what it means, Greg."

Tracy glanced over at Greg. He was leaning against the pueblo wall, taking in everything. A cold smile flickered across his face. "It means you've done it again, Doc," he said. "You'll get credit for turning back the Southwest time line and proving that some of your rivals are way off base."

Doc smacked his fist against the palm of his hand. "Exactly! And the best part is that we've only begun. When I look across this plain and think of all the civilizations buried beneath the grass, I get goosebumps."

Ray threw back his head and laughed. "Does he scare you, Tracy? I'll bet you didn't know that Doc dreams of digging up all the land as far as the eye can see."

Tracy returned his grin. "I wouldn't mind, provided I can rest in between bouts."

"If it's a rest you want, you'll get that right away," Doc said. "Now that this burial's complete, I'm shipping you back to the lab to catalog everything. Greg'll help you."

Tracy stiffened. The others failed to notice as they talked around her. Ignored, she set about shifting the bowls from the grave floor to the boxes. She picked up the McDonald and gently pried loose a thick clod of soil blocking its mouth. After wrapping it in newsprint, she reached for the Tularosa. Unlike the heavy clay blocking the interior of the first pot, the dirt filling its cavity was loose and easy to dislodge. As she upended the bowl, she heard a distinct rattle from within. Thrusting her hand inside, she felt a smooth narrow circlet. Slowly, she drew it out into the bright sunlight and stared at it, transfixed. "Oooh," she breathed.

The others crowded close to see the bone bracelet she held. Belying its primitive origin, it was adorned by an enormous turquoise stone set in a thick section of bone that had been painstakingly carved until it provided a secure setting for the gem.

Doc stared at the bracelet. Even the wind, normally brisk and wild in its incessant sweep across the plain, paused in its passage, seeming to hover directly above the knot of motionless observers. Tracy felt transported to a bygone moment. She envisioned an adventuresome artisan, inspired to experiment with stones roughly strewn at his feet by nature, crafting a design destined to be perfected by his silversmith descendants.

Doc whistled through his teeth, breaking the spell. "Unbelievable!" Plucking the bracelet from Tracy's hand, he turned it from side to side, as if half expecting it to self-destruct. "We'll call this the Reynolds Turquoise. It's only right, isn't that so, Greg?"

His eyes narrowing, Greg mumbled something noncommittal. Inexplicably, Tracy shivered, but the very next moment the joy of her discovery and the splendid warmth of the sun filled her heart. Once again, she laughed and chatted easily.

By the time the artifacts were loaded into the truck and the box containing the precious turquoise bracelet was safely up front on Doc's lap, she put aside all thought except her gnawing hunger and the promise of Clarence's delicious meal at the end of the trail.

Chapter 11

Tracy's burial was the center of all conversations that evening, but Doc made certain to halt any resentment that might be brewing by assuring everyone that the find could not be an isolated incident.

"We're bound to uncover many more treasures by summer's end," he said. "To hurry up the process, I'm transferring some of you who are working on strat tests to the broadside."

Bill leaned over to Tracy. "He means that we're working against time. Once the locals learn about the turquoise, they'll sneak onto the site when nobody's around and try to find more. We have to beat them to it."

Tracy shot him a worried glance. "You think that could happen?" She had watched the Apache cowboys drive their cattle across the range every day, but none seemed particularly interested in the camp operations.

Bill shrugged. "Wouldn't you, if you were in their shoes? After all, everything here belongs to them. I doubt they'd feel any remorse about taking what their ancestors made."

Tracy became wistful. "I wish I could stay on the site."

"You'll be back out there as soon as you finish your lab work."

"That's not the only reason for doing it quickly." She spoke more to herself than to Bill.

Tracy's concerns faded soon after she settled into the lab. Greg was seldom around because Doc needed him at the dig. Her initial task, labeling all she had uncovered on the broadside, was easy enough. Once that was done, there remained the chore of packing everything, carefully padding each piece to withstand the rough truck ride back to the university museum.

Even before Tracy's first full day in the lab ended, Brenda and Shirley Morgan joined her. Since they were being moved to the broadside, they had come to catalogue the results of their strat test. Cheered by the prospect of duplicating Tracy's discovery, they burrowed busily into their task. Tracy was grateful for their silence.

It was nearly time to break for supper when Snakeskin burst in. "Where's Doc?"

Tracy scarcely glanced up. "No idea."

"He was on his way to Forestdale the last we saw him," Shirley said.

"Then he hasn't heard!" Grinning like a mountain lion with a full stomach, Snakeskin plopped onto a table top and fanned himself with his ten-gallon hat. "Will he be surprised!"

That caught Brenda's attention. "What are you talking about?"

"More turquoise. Diane found another bracelet. Right near where you found yours, Tracy. It wasn't in a burial, though. Just tossed onto the trash pile."

Tracy was genuinely pleased for Diane. "Doc felt sure more would turn up. It's only logical that the person who made my bracelet wouldn't stop at one piece of jewelry."

Shirley agreed. "Judging by the one you found, he must have practiced on others first to work out the best technique."

"Don't get your hopes up about finding more," Snakeskin cautioned. "It could happen, but there's a lot of earth out there to be moved, and the chances of hitting the right spots are slim."

"Still, two so near each other could indicate there's more where they came from," Tracy said.

"Time will tell," Snakeskin said, as he headed to the supply cabinet and retrieved a roll of film. "I almost forgot why I came. I have to photograph the turquoise *in situ* right now so we can bring it in. It wouldn't do to leave it there overnight. Diane's still waiting for me at the broadside, but I brought the others back so they won't be late for supper. If Doc shows up, tell him we'll be back soon with a surprise."

"Will do," Tracy said.

"What kind of surprise?" Greg had managed to enter the lab without allowing the screen door to creak like a chirping cricket.

"Pussyfooting again, are you?" Snakeskin voiced Tracy's very thought. "Another hunk of turquoise out at the broadside."

Greg's eyebrows shot up. "You think it's authentic?"

"As authentic as anything buried under six feet of soil. I'm bringing it in as soon as I get a photo."

"I'll be glad to go along and help," Greg said.

Tracy thought Greg seemed a little too eager. She was thankful that Snakeskin put him off tactfully.

"No need. The sun's still at a decent angle on that part of the broadside and Diane's there. We shouldn't run into a problem that can't be handled by two heads."

"You're probably right," Greg conceded, as he turned his attention to Tracy's sheets. She caught her breath, expecting him to find fault, but he waved away her fears with a half smile. "Looks good. That's enough for now. You'd better get ready for supper."

Tracy was certain he was preoccupied with Snakeskin's announcement rather than her notes. She saw his jaw twitch as he watched Snakeskin swing up into the truck cab. The thought crossed her mind that he might be planning to steal the jewel. More than once she had seen him conferring with tribal members passing through camp. Now she wondered if he had made a deal to return their ancestors' valuables for some kind of exchange.

All of her instincts shouted that Greg was a man to be watched carefully, and she vowed to do all she could to uncover whatever evil plot he had concocted. Since he was the only one at camp no longer directly connected with the university, she believed that he was the most logical one to err from the straight and narrow for either personal profit or fame.

As Tracy slipped out the screen door, Greg moved toward the table where Brenda and Shirley were still cataloguing their finds. Momentarily, she heard him exclaim, "Oh, for Pete's sake! This won't do. Your numbers aren't legible. This page has to be redone."

Relieved that he was on someone else's case, not hers, Tracy closed him out of her thoughts the moment she caught sight of Bill waving from the Forestdale truck. She waved back cheerfully, then jogged to her cabin to freshen up for supper. The shaded path, thickly strewn with pine needles, was somehow soothing, an anodyne to the tedious cataloguing. The sweet, pungent pine scent permeated the air as always, yet now it seemed more insistent, more oppressive.

Tracy snatched up a fresh change of clothing and headed for the bathhouse, quickening her pace as the tantalizing aroma of bread baking reminded her that she had not eaten for many hours. A shower and shampoo accomplished, she slipped into a blouse and full skirt and brushed her hair until it gleamed.

Feeling feminine for the first time in weeks, she lingered several moments at the mirror in anticipation of the square dance Snakeskin had planned for the evening, a welcome change from the physical and mental strain of the past few weeks.

Because the early rising schedule allowed no time for primping, Tracy had limited her daily makeup routine to a rosy slash of lipstick. For this occasion, she planned to add a few more cosmetic touches, but a swift examination of her reflection confirmed that nothing else was necessary. Her complexion, bronzed by the sun, was a perfect base for cheeks that glowed pink.

"This place is exactly like a health spa," she said to Iris, who had moved alongside to examine herself critically in the mirror.

"Now I know the sun has gone to your head," Iris said. "When we ride back to camp every afternoon, I feel that the end is nigh. We might as well be piled up in those medieval carts drawn by a serf chanting, 'Bring out your dead.'"

Tracy laughed aloud. "Oh, Iris! You wake me up, no matter how tired I am. With your help, I may even make it through the square dance. How about you?"

"I have no high hopes about my own energy supply, but Bill's bound to be after you all evening, so you'll have no trouble keeping the blood circulating."

Tracy blushed and floundered before replying. "He's not the kind of energy source I need. Compared with other men I know, he's much too pushy. Unfortunately, we exist in close quarters at camp. There aren't many opportunities to escape him without being rude. Instead of carrying on a normal conversation, he talks on and on about how we'll be inseparable in the fall when I'm working at the university. I've learned absolutely nothing about him except through offhanded remarks, mostly about the excavations at Forestville. His intentions may be honorable, but I don't like that kind of pressure."

Iris nodded. "I know exactly what you mean. Still, he's a great looking guy. You know what they say about turning down a gift horse."

"I came here for experience in the field, remember? Digging up a man was not on my agenda."

"That's what they all say. Me, I'm different. You could say I'm a throwback to a luxury-loving generation. Preparing for an exciting career is nice as far as it goes, but if I could dig up Mr. Right as easily as you seem to do, I'd willingly chuck the dirt, the aches and pains, and the books for a nice house in the suburbs, a television, a garden I can putter in to my heart's content, and season theater tickets. What I crave right now are city lights. I never thought I'd be so deprived of culture that I'd look forward to a country hoedown for entertainment."

Tracy laughed. "I've heard it takes a couple of months to adjust to the simple life."

"Maybe that's time enough for you, but I'm a lost cause," Iris said. "Now will you please quit fooling with your hair! You look better than anyone else here without half trying. That kind of competition I don't need."

Even before arriving at the dance, they were snapping their fingers to the infectious strains of Clarence's fiddle pouring from the open windows. Within a few minutes, Tracy observed, Iris had left her pessimism in the bathhouse and was reliving her prom queen days. When she wasn't whirling through a Texas star with the Psi Theta boys, she was clapping up a storm with the camp veterans responding to Snakeskin's calls.

No longer concerned about her friend, Tracy entered into the spirit, moving rapidly from one partner to another to avoid the worry of having to cope with Bill. She had just begun to loosen up when the Virginia Reel began and Doc chose her to join him at the head. She hesitated. The last thing she wanted to do was cause Julia to smolder on the sidelines, but Julia surprised her. Instead of glowering, she smiled and waved Tracy onto the floor, saying. "Have fun. Perspiration's not my favorite partner."

Released from the fear of causing undue trouble through no fault of her own, Tracy accepted Doc's proffered hand and followed him into position for the reel. He proved to be as expert on the dance floor as he was in the classroom or out in the field. How, she wondered, could one man be so perfect in so many areas? He swept her from one end of the room to the other as if powered by a generator, never missing a step and maintaining a demanding pace throughout. As Clarence took his final licks on the fiddle, she congratulated herself silently for surviving, but the intricate steps of the next dance, "Put Your Little Foot," required more dexterity than she could summon. Excusing herself, she sank down beside Julia.

Julia flashed a conspiratorial smile and squeezed her hand. "You're a trouper," she said. "I could tell that you were winding down, but you kept at it."

Tracy returned the smile. "You're right. It's not easy keeping up with Doc. He has more pep than all of us put together. You were wise to sit it out and save your energy."

Julia looked her straight in the eye. "A lot of good that does me. The fact is that energy is not what I need. I have plenty of that, but no way to spend it. At one point, I made a list of dozens of things I'd love to do, but when I showed it to Doc, he told me they were out of the question. My wishes don't matter. That's why I have to keep coming here with him each summer. It's certainly not my idea of a vacation."

Tracy wanted to be sympathetic. "It must be hard on you, especially since you have to amuse yourself while we're out on the dig all day long."

"You do understand, don't you, Tracy? I can read just so many cheap novels and write so many letters. I can't describe how much I miss going shopping and meeting friends for the afternoon. The only consolation is that being here is better than sitting at home wondering …"

"About what?" Tracy wanted to take back those words the moment she blurted them out. She felt herself turning crimson.

Julia measured Tracy swiftly. Without losing a beat, she replied, "About Doc, and when this all will end, and why I put up with it."

"Oh, but I …" Tracy began. Defensive, she believed Julia was accusing her of trifling with Doc's affections.

Julia's laugh was mirthless. "I'm afraid that I'm confusing you. You're too serious, maybe even too smart, but I've been watching you and I have to warn you that you're not smart enough to see through the camouflage. You're also not smart enough to recognize a good man when he's right under your nose."

Tracy stiffened. "Bill is a nice enough guy, but I don't know much about him and I really don't want him to think that I'm interested in him any way other than as a friend. My reason for being here is to learn all I can so I walk into my new job understanding every process connected with field research."

"Bill?" Julia looked confused. "Oh, no. I meant …"

"Did someone mention my name?" Whatever Julia was about to say was lost forever as Bill bounded up, pulled Tracy to her feet, and led her onto the dance floor.

That was as far as they got. Hands on her hips, Tracy stopped dead in the middle of the floor and confronted him. "You might at least have the courtesy of asking. The truth is, I would have preferred sitting this one out. In any event, I don't appreciate being dragged away when I'm in the middle of a conversation."

Bill grinned. "I thought we knew each another well enough to skip the formalities."

"It would pay you to learn that a woman appreciates the little niceties," Tracy said.

"In that case, let me apologize for interrupting. I didn't know that you were close friends with Julia."

"I know her as well as I know you, maybe better," Tracy said. "The point is, you were rude."

Bill bowed low. "Yes, master. I admit that I was rude. Now will you please give me the pleasure of this dance?"

Tracy sighed. She realized that there was a pause in the music and others were looking in their direction expectantly. Succumbing to Bill's penitent grin, she let him propel her toward three couples in need of a fourth for their square.

As they took their places, he whispered into her ear, "Deep down in your heart, I'll bet you prefer the caveman type who hauls you away to his lair. And to keep you from being disappointed, I warn you that I plan to spirit you away after the dance. Just you and me all alone in the wide open spaces."

Tracy regarded him icily. "Don't count on it."

As the first few bars of music rollicked around the room, Bill hugged Tracy on the pretext of positioning her for the dance. She opened her mouth to protest, but nothing came out, for at that very instant, the gong outside began to knell.

On signal, the room became deathly still, as if someone had turned a giant key, stifling the voices that only seconds before were chattering amiably and shackling the hands that had been clapping in time to the infectious rhythms.

Snakeskin on his guitar and Clarence on an ancient fiddle had just struck up a tune. Now their hands were poised in mid-air.

The second gong reverberated through the camp. Three ... four ... five rang out, the dreaded warning of a forest fire. Just at the remarkable second when every neck was craned instinctively toward the door, it burst open, the entranceway blocked by a formidable figure.

Chapter 12

It was Greg. That was a given. During the square dance, Tracy realized he was the only camp member not present. Even before he dominated the room, brushing aside everyone in his path to reach Doc, it was clear that Greg was the bearer of bad news. Why, Tracy wondered, had she not recognized the subtle warning earlier? The acrid odor permeating the air must have come from smoldering brush on a nearby mountain, its smoke funneled across the plateau by the driving winds.

After a swift exchange with Greg, Doc raised his hand for attention. "We've just had a call from Ranger Newman. He says there's a blaze out of control over near Gila Peak. They need a back-up crew, all the men we can spare, so that means all except Woody, Greg, and Clarence …"

Greg interrupted Doc in a low, intense voice. At the close of their heated exchange, Doc nodded reluctantly. "Greg will go to the fire, and I'll stay here—to keep an eye on the lovely ladies." Tracy interpreted his broad wink as a way of calming fears. "We'll need about four vehicles. Ray, Snakeskin, Joe—can you help us out?" Each nodded solemnly as Doc continued. "We'll load up water barrels, buckets, and shovels. Don't forget your canteens. Clarence, can we have enough food for a few days?"

Clarence, already anticipating the request, waved his hand in assent and disappeared into the kitchen.

"Be ready to leave in fifteen minutes," Doc said, adding. "Tracy, you're in charge of the lab."

Before Tracy could blink, Diane leaned over to sympathize. "Poor you. He's handed you a thankless package."

Tracy forgot about herself when she glanced around and saw Marie's face. "What's wrong, Marie?"

"It's Ray. He shouldn't go up there. He has asthma. That's why his family moved to Arizona. Nobody else knows. He's been fine for years, but it might start up again if he breathes the smoke. I know he won't speak up for the world because he thinks it's his duty to go. If he dies fighting on an obscure mountain, people will say what a hero he was and forget all about him the next day. You read about such things all the time."

"If you're that worried, say something to Doc."

"And have Ray furious with me for making him look like a coward?"

Tracy tried to be optimistic. "The fire may amount to nothing. They could be back here by dawn."

"I wish I believed you," Marie said. "Some forest fires are stubborn. They can drag on for weeks."

"Volunteers aren't expected to work that long, are they?"

"It all depends on the kind of fire it is and how soon replacements arrive." Marie's voice dropped to a whisper. "I'm so worried, Tracy."

"We have to believe that everything will work out," Tracy said, flashing her friend what she hoped was a consoling smile; she merely succeeded in feeling as if her own shoulders were supporting more troubles than they could handle.

Not long after Tracy returned to her cabin, Doc sent Stu with word that more blankets were needed. "I'll take whatever you can spare," Stu said.

Even though nights in the high country could be bitter cold, Tracy gladly sacrificed a blanket, hoping it would cushion one of the men forced to sleep on the hard ground.

Stu smile gratefully as Tracy folded and piled her blanket on top of the others in his arms. The stack he amassed was so high he could barely peer over the top.

"Be sure you don't get mine dirty," Iris cautioned, with a laugh. "You may be indebted to me for life."

"Fat chance," Stu said, not pausing to linger for his usual friendly banter.

"I've never known the rangers to ask the camp for help," Diane said, as those left behind stood in a somber circle watching the men prepare to leave. "The fire threat's been real every summer, but I never thought any of us actually would use our training on the front line."

Facial expressions all around matched hers in seriousness, except for the wide grin Bill sported as he bounded up to Tracy. "Aren't you going to kiss me goodbye? After all, I'm going off to battle."

Tracy replied with a long, hard stare. "If I accommodate you, then I'll have to oblige the others, and I doubt that Doc wants you men to waste any more time."

"Just one kiss," Bill begged, in mock dismay.

Firmly, Tracy said, "It will keep."

Greg swung into his truck. "Let's go, Harrison," he growled. As he switched on the ignition, the other drivers followed suit.

Within moments, all four vehicles were moving up the track toward the plateau, their headlights piercing the thick pines until their branches, magnified, were splayed across the camp building like zombies rising from the earth. The trucks crawled single file up the slope toward the dig site, but once on level ground, they veered directly across the plain toward Kinishba Ridge. There they would pick up the gravel road coursing from the Salt River Canyon to the base of the Gila Mountains. At length, the last red taillight flickered, and was gone.

There was no word the next day, or the day after that, only the pungent smell wafting down from the heights to remind those below of the absent men. If Tracy had taken R. J., Stu, Joe, and Red for granted during her early days at camp, she now viewed them—along with the kitchen crew—as no less vital members of the group than Ray, Snakeskin, and Bill. She was astounded by the rapid, mysterious way they had gripped her mind and heart. Even Greg left a curious void in her life.

"I'm almost beginning to miss his complaints," Iris said.

Without pausing to weigh her words, Tracy said, "You can't miss him as much as I do. I'm going crazy with all the work in this lab. Doc is no help because he's gone all day at the sites. I never thought I'd see the time when I'd welcome Greg back with open arms." She laughed, embarrassed by her admission. "Well, almost. The minute he's back, I'll be free of this ball and chain of a lab. I'd give anything to be back out on the dig and I don't care where Doc puts me next. Any place is better than being cooped up here with tons of paper work and thousands of tiny broken pieces to catalog."

Marie grow more listless and aloof by the hour. Tracy was not surprised when Becky told her that Marie spent the night shuffling across the wooden floor of their cabin to peer out the window and scan the horizon.

At that point, Tracy decided that someone needed to be assertive. "Marie, you can't go on like this. I'm going to ask Doc if we can drive his truck to Gila Peak to look for the men."

Marie resisted until it became clear to her that Tracy meant business. Together they approached Doc. He was sympathetic, but adamant.

"Absolutely not! Greg and Snakeskin know what they're doing. They won't let the others get into dangerous situations. Furthermore, there's no way you two could help them. They'll be back when the job is done, but if you get lost or injured on the way up, there's nobody in camp to go after you. I'm in charge, so I have no choice. Woody has to stay here in case someone gets sick or has an accident. I'm sorry, Marie, but that's out." Moved by several tears rolling down her cheek, he added, "I'm betting they return by tomorrow. I heard over the radio that the rangers asked the government to send professional fighters. The replacements should arrive in a matter of hours."

Tracy and Marie retreated to the kitchen where Becky had volunteered to help Clarence while Jerry, Mack, and Ed were away. "Grab aprons for yourselves and start scraping plates," Becky said. "Three pairs of hands can wash these dishes in no time. This may be a time for sacrifice, but it's kind of a nice change for me to be excused from the broadside."

Tracy shifted easily into the kitchen detail, wiping the dishes and utensils Becky scrubbed before passing them along so Marie could return them to the proper drawers and shelves. "Do you trust Diane and Rosa to cover your job there along with their own?"

"It's not a matter of trust, but of pleasing Doc," Becky said. "I think his goal is to expose enough rooms in the pueblo by the end of summer for Juniper Junction to qualify as a national monument."

"Even if he succeeds, this place is so far off the beaten path, tourists would never find their way," Marie said.

Tracy nodded. "That's probably the best thing that could happen to a national monument. If nobody comes, there's no chance someone could damage it out of either spite or stupidity. Still, it's a marvelous site that's becoming more photogenic by the day."

"A lot better by far than Forestdale," Becky said. "Now there's a challenge I don't care to take."

"Me neither," Marie agreed. "It must date back centuries earlier than the pueblo. Ray told me that the winds sweeping across the plateau had buried the rooms under such thick layers of soil that some are far below ground level. To reach them, the men have to climb down a series of ladders. It takes forever to excavate the rooms because the low man down has to shovel each bucket full of dirt."

"Wow!" Becky exclaimed. "Then what?"

Marie continued. "Then it's hand-hoisted along a human chain to the man at the surface, like our fire brigade. The job of the man on top is to carry each bucket as far away from the area as he can manage so the pile doesn't interfere with future work."

"That's intense labor, for sure," Tracy said. "No matter how eager we are to help, we lack the muscle power."

"And don't forget the rattlesnakes," Becky said.

Tracy groaned. "Enough said. Snakeskin's daily reports of close encounters almost make my lab assignment palatable."

Back in the lab, the hours dragged as Tracy catalogued and packed the pottery, tools, and jewelry for the museum while listening for the approaching trucks. With every unannounced crunch of footsteps on gravel and each creak of the porch floorboards, Tracy jumped with anticipation. She was alone in camp, except for Julia in her own private world, Clarence and Becky in the kitchen, and Woody, who remained in the infirmary, aloof and unapproachable. As she worked, she recalled a remark Becky made the first day she began helping in the kitchen.

"I'd better not cut myself with a paring knife because I seriously doubt Woody's ability to dress a wound," Becky had said. "In fact, I find it hard to believe he's a legitimate doctor."

Becky's skepticism was nourished by an earlier encounter with him when the safety pins dangling from her earlobes caused an infection. Wide-eyed, she reported afterwards to Tracy that Woody merely glanced at her before suggesting, with an ugly scowl, that she have her ears amputated.

Tracy assured Becky that Woody was trying to make a joke. Secretly, she doubted her own words. She persuaded Becky to remove the pins and treat the infection with medicine from her own first-aid kit. Once Becky's ears began to heal, Tracy intended to mention the incident to Doc, but never did.

She was bent over the table trying to cement together pieces of a jar when she heard footsteps mounting the porch stairs. Believing that the men were back, she let the shards clatter to the table and rushed to the door. Instead of the men, she faced a small, shy Apache woman. Tracy sucked in a deep breath to stifle her disappointment. "How can I help you?"

Hesitating before Tracy, as if expecting to be greeted by someone else, the woman shuffled from one softly booted foot to the other and wiped her perspiring hands against her stained skirt. Her high cheekbones accented smooth, youthful skin, but the deep-set eyes were filled with unfathomable cisterns of ancient knowledge. Tracy could not begin to judge the woman's age.

The visitor drew a small packet from a deep slit in her skirt and handed it to Tracy. "The doctor wants this," she said.

"Doc's out in the field now, but I'll be glad to give it to him later."

The women frowned. "You sure?"

"Of course. Most of the men have gone to fight a forest fire, so I can't leave the lab now, but I'll put this in a safe place and give it to him when he comes back."

"Yes, my men are away, too. I came because he wanted this soon."

Tracy felt it was none of her business to ask what the package held, but she could not resist succumbing to curiosity. "How did you get here?"

"I walked."

"From the village down the road?"

The woman nodded.

"It's a shame you had to travel so far in this heat. Can I get you a drink of water?"

The woman shook her head, but made no move to leave. She stood quietly n the doorway until Tracy remembered the package still in her hand. It seemed weightless. "I'm sorry. I should have asked if there is a bill for this."

"A bill?" The woman seemed puzzled.

"I mean, does Doc owe you anything for this?"

The woman brightened. "Oh no. He paid already. That's why I came. So he's not mad. He doesn't like to wait."

Tracy smiled. "You don't need to worry about that. Doc never gets mad. I promise to give it to him when he comes back."

That seemed to satisfy the woman. As silently as she had come, she turned and stepped away into the bright sunlight.

To make certain that the parcel was stored in a safe spot and not misplaced among the pile of objects she was indexing, Tracy opened the desk drawer and tucked it beneath Greg's ledger. As her hand brushed its cover, she was tempted to leaf through the pages, but she hesitated. She could almost feel his steely eyes burning through her back all the way from the forest fire.

Everyone in camp understood that Greg's ledger was off limits, purportedly to insure an accurate account of the dig. Tracy saw no reason for his fanatic secrecy. Each person compiled and submitted a log to Greg. He, in turn, entered the findings in the ledger in his own hand. This part of the routine made sense to Tracy because it ensured that the ledger conformed to scientific standards. Next to Doc, Greg was the only one in the group familiar with the meticulous requirements of university archives. Still, she did not understand why others were prohibited from reading his entries. It would be a good way, she philosophized, to learn the acceptable format.

The restriction struck her as so arbitrary that she did something she never, ever believed herself capable of doing. Throwing all honor to the wind, she cracked the cover ever so slightly, telling herself she intended only to study the procedure she would be expected to master in her new job.

The ledger fell open to a date just prior to the day she unearthed the Reynolds Turquoise. Unable to quell her urges, she allowed her eyes to scan the next few sheets in quest of the entry that would verify her find.

"Odd," she said, aloud.

The two bowls were recorded, but not the bracelet. Even if Greg had filed a separate report on the bracelet, she felt certain it should be included among the list of grave furniture.

Unduly disturbed, she began leafing through the pages beyond. Surely she could find the missing entry. Nothing.

She sat up with a jerk. Now that she knew the oversight was deliberate, she was determined to pursue the matter. Rushing to the corner of the room where Greg had stacked the boxes of materials from her site, she found the one that logic dictated should hold the bracelet. Beginning on the top layer, she worked her way through the collection, unwrapping each bone, each pottery shard. At last, all lay bare on the table. Mounds of newsprint billowed at her feet.

Now it was clear! Her turquoise bracelet was not entered in Greg's ledger for the simple reason that it had been removed—stolen?—by someone with motives less than honorable. To think she had worried so about prying into his sacred ledger!

Mindful of the anger swirling within her, Tracy deliberately re-wrapped every piece. She repacked the box with such care that the most suspicious detective could not sense her intrusion into forbidden territory. The only way to fight deceit, she concluded, was with deceit.

After working off her fury by straightening up the lab, organizing cartons of pottery, bones, and rocks to be catalogued and packed, and penciling memos to herself for the next day, she headed for the showers, hoping that a shampoo would wash away the mean streak that had surfaced within her upon discovering Greg's deception.

Chapter 13

The pure mountain water produced alpine heaps of suds. After bathing and dressing in a fresh outfit, Tracy stepped into a pool of afternoon sun. As her hair dried, it fell about her face in soft ringlets. So, too, did her temper soften. Tucking away her rancor into the recesses of her mind, she directed her attention to the delicious aromas drifting from the kitchen.

She strolled to the edge of camp and mounted the ridge, expecting to see the truck rumbling back from the dig. Shielding her eyes, she saw forms still moving about the broadside while Doc waited for everyone to polish off notes and gather up the gear. She was about to turn back to camp when a wispy cloud moving imperceptibly along the base of the mountain caught her attention.

She felt her stomach jolt, for the specter of fire had been her constant companion since the men left camp, but as the cloud reached a break in the pines, she caught a glint of sun on steel. The flash lasted for a brief second. It was followed by another, then another.

"The trucks!" she cried to the earth, the sky and the mute, ancient gods, for nobody else could hear. "The men are coming!"

Tracy sprinted back to the dining hall, slamming the screen door with enough force to unnerve Clarence, who nearly dropped the roasting pan he was lifting from the oven.

He admonished her sternly. "Whoa, young lady! If you want your dinner, you'd better slow down. There's a cake in there, too. If it falls, you'll sit in the corner all evening."

"Oh, Clarence, your food's marvelous whether it's upside down or right-side up, but you'd better have enough to feed the men because I see them coming."

Catching the excitement in her voice, Clarence set the pan down, put his hands on his hips, and gave her one of his you-should-know-better looks. "You'd better believe I can feed everyone. But if we run short, you won't mind donating you share, will you?"

"Not if I can have a slice of your pecan bread right now," she said, admiring the golden loaves cooling on wire racks.

"You trying to get fat, girl? Pretty soon you'll be as beefy as the cattle out on the range. Of course the more meat there is on your bones, the more work you can do for Doc."

Tracy grinned back at him as he held the knife in the air to tantalize and force her to beg for his succulent specialty. "Anyone who cooks for a football squad knows that people use up more calories at high altitudes. Besides, I'll work it off in a single morning out on the dig." Then she threw in her trump card. "I'll even give you a hand tonight if you need extra help."

"You are one terrific salesperson," Clarence conceded. He sliced an ambrosial chunk before motioning Tracy to the apron rack.

Following Clarence's cursory directions and Becky's example, Tracy slipped neatly into the kitchen routine. By the time the first truck rumbled down the gravel trace into camp, the tables were set, the sideboard was spread with delectable breads, preserves, and salad fixings, and the cauldrons on the range bubbled with intoxicating medleys of squash, corn, and tomatoes, honorable accompaniments to the roast beef.

The sound of boots mounting the dining hall steps quickly propelled Tracy into the dining room. She expected a stampede, but it was only Jerry. Filthy and haggard, he appeared far older than his sixteen years.

Tracy spoke casually to mask her astonishment at his appearance. "Where is everybody? I thought you'd all be hungry as thieves."

"Greg sent me to tell Clarence we're heading for the showers first. Don't you think I could use one?" Jerry's slow grin told Tracy that he had weathered the experience well.

"Is … is everyone all right?"

He shrugged. "Guess so. Say, are you trying to snatch away my job?"

"For today only, I can assure you. I promise you can have it back tomorrow."

"I'm in no hurry," Jerry said. "Give me a chance to get some sleep. The way I feel now, I may not be able to keep my eyes open during supper."

"When you see what Clarence has fixed, I think you'll do it justice. See you when you're ready," Tracy said, as Jerry retreated down the steps.

"See ya," he called over his shoulder. He struck out across the piney path wearing the air of a child-soldier returning from battle transformed into a man.

Just then, the stake truck rolled into camp, Doc at the wheel. The cheers of the field crew crowded around the rails contrasted eerily with the silent, unsmiling men unloading their trucks. Snakeskin and Greg were pitching bundles to the Psi Theta boys, who stacked them neatly on the ground. The moment Ray caught sight of Marie, he ran headlong to meet her. They held each other for a long time before pulling apart and commencing an animated exchange. Tracy was relieved that Bill was nowhere to be seen. She was not ready to handle a reunion, especially the emotional one he might try to promote.

Doc and Greg conferred for a few moments before the older man threw his arm impetuously around the shoulder of the younger and gave him a great bear hug. Tracy was reminded of a football coach extending congratulations to a player whose remarkable run climaxed in the end zone. She watched them move down the path together, an oddly compatible pair in appearance. Both were tall and athletically built, Greg moving with the sleek grace of a young panther, Doc effused with the pride and assurance of a mature lion. She was struck with the thought that they were at once alike, yet opposite, one outgoing and beloved, the other moving through life's shadows surreptitiously, almost as if he were entrusted with a secret mission.

Remembering the message for Clarence, Tracy wheeled about and ran to the kitchen where he was busy carving the roast. He accepted Jerry's communication with his usual calm, then instructed her to help Becky transfer the meat to a hot platter. "That has to stay warm until the men are ready to polish it off," he said. "Take care you pay attention so it doesn't slide onto the floor. I don't have an emergency replacement in the pantry."

Tracy and Becky were congratulating themselves for executing the transfer without a hitch when Marie burst into the kitchen.

"You were right, Tracy! It all worked out fine."

"The smoke didn't bother Ray?"

"Yes, and no. Just as soon as he began coughing, Greg ordered him off the front line. Ray spent the rest of his time relaying radio messages. He finally managed to get through to the right people to order replacements, or they wouldn't be back here yet. Our men and a few from the Indian village had to contain the fire by themselves until a new contingent could be flown in. Something else, too … Ray says your Bill was an absolute coward."

Tracy bristled. "*My* Bill! He's no such thing, simply a friend, nothing more. You should know that much. But what do you mean by a coward?"

"Apparently Bill kept sneaking away and leaving all the tough work for the young kids from the kitchen. They did all right without him, it turned out. Ray also said that the Psi Theta guys showed a lot of guts. Hung in there the whole time. Pretty surprising for rich kids. Of course, most of the load fell on Snakeskin and Greg. Ray said that Greg finally lost his temper and hung one on Bill when he caught him ducking out once too often."

Tracy suppressed a smile. "So that's why Bill wasn't so quick about coming around to collect a kiss. What you've just told me gives a good reason for delaying his pleasure. Thanks for sharing. Say, if you plan to dress for supper, you'd better hurry. If those men are as ravenous as I think they'll be, there won't be much left after the first round."

"Good point." Marie wheeled around and headed for the showers. It was obvious to Tracy that Marie's heart was lighter than it had been the night the men left.

The supper, speedily consumed, was remarkable for the silence punctuating the clink of silverware upon dishes, ladles scraping the bottoms of deep tureens, and knives slicing through thick, crusty bread.

Each person was careful to avoid discussing the topic on everyone's mind.

Tracy listened while Iris, Diane, and Rosa chatted about their day on the broadside, comparing notes with Brenda and Shirley, whose strat test had not produced one encouraging shard of pottery. They talked as animatedly as women can about dirt, bones and clay containers, all the while casting covert glances at the faces of the men who downed heaping servings without comment.

Nobody seemed surprised by Tracy's new role until she began clearing the head table. Glancing up, Doc said, "You're a multi-talented woman if I ever saw one. What can't you do?"

Tracy smiled. "That's a book in itself." For Doc's ears only, she added, "Actually, I'm not cut out for lab work and I hope you'll pull me off duty there now that Mr. Director is back."

Doc raised his eyebrows. "You're not happy in the lab? That's a pity. Greg says you do an excellent job. In fact, he convinced me to put you there."

Greg, seated next to Doc, said nothing, but Tracy noticed a flicker of amusement around his mouth. She could scarcely conceal her triumph when their eyes met and he choked on a swallow of coffee.

Doc, unable to observe the silent exchange, continued innocently. "But since you want to get back out on the dig, I don't see why you can't start there tomorrow morning. That is, if things are up to date in the lab." As he spoke, Doc searched for the butter dish and finding it, hacked off a chunk nearly the thickness of the slab of bread he sought to spread. "You can fill Greg in on anything that needs to be done."

"I believe he'll find everything to his liking," Tracy said. Deliberately, she projected her remark toward Greg, careful to avert her eyes from his. She fully intended to confront him about her missing turquoise, but this was not the appropriate time and place.

From across the room, Bill watched her steadily. Tracy wondered if he feared they were discussing his behavior at the fire. She was thankful that Becky was serving his table. By keeping her distance, she could prolong a point-blank reunion.

As soon as supper ended, well before the dessert dishes were cleared away, the men left. Tracy presumed that most planned to catch up on several days' sleep; in Bill's case, she suspected it was to avoid embarrassment. Once she and Becky finished helping Clarence tidy the kitchen and set up everything needed for breakfast, they joined Iris and Marie on the circular wooden bench that wrapped around a great tree in front of the dining hall. On previous evenings, Snakeskin had dropped by with his guitar and they had sung until bedtime. Left to their own devices, they barely managed a few familiar folk songs, Iris adding a harmony of a sort in what she liked to call her basso-alto, but the spontaneity and fun they enjoyed in the past when the men chimed in was missing. They soon dissolved their unlikely quartet and headed for the cabins.

Diane chuckled as she slipped into her sleeping bag. "Did you see that shiner on Bill?"

"He must have run into a tree," Brenda said, panting, as she faithfully executed her nightly exercise routine.

Or a mountain of trouble, Tracy thought. Aloud, she said, "Oh, rats!" She began to pull on the boots she had tossed under her cot.

Diane took immediate notice. "Forget to kiss Bill goodnight to make it well?"

"Don't be idiotic, Diane. It so happens that I left my log book in the lab and I'll need it tomorrow if Doc sends me out on the dig. There's always such a mad dash in the morning, I'll forget it for sure. I'd better get it now."

"Watch out for snakes," Iris cautioned. An evil that had never plagued her in the city had become an obsession.

"There's more than one kind of snake in camp," Diane said, rolling over. "Douse that light on the way out, will you, Tracy?"

"Done," Tracy called, closing the door as she left.

The absence of the moon magnified the stars twinkling through the tops of the pines until she almost believed she could touch them. As she proceeded down the familiar pathway, the feathery branches of the junipers brushed against her arms. The camp lay dark and still in all directions; not one flashlight beam announced a lone visitor to the Green Kiva. Even the faint line of demarcation between Kinishba Ridge and the sky, ordinarily visible, was missing.

Tracy padded noiselessly across the pine needle carpet until she reached the crest of the gravel sweep. There she cut across the grass, already sodden with evening dew, and mounted the steps to the lab, careful to prevent her boots from clattering on the wood and reverberating across camp to waken the men who needed to make up their lost sleep.

The latch turned readily and the door creaked open. Tracy stepped warily across the threshold, groping along the wall. Just as her hand located the light switch, her sixth sense flashed a warning: another presence hovered nearby. She caught her breath, terrified, but before she could react to her intuition and retreat from danger, a powerful hand grasped her wrist, wrenching her off balance.

The cry beginning to well up in her throat was muffled the moment her face smashed into a solid wall of chest. She struggled to free herself, but her assailant pinned her arms behind her back, pressing her head so firmly into a thick wool sweater that Tracy believed he was trying to smother her. In defense, she resorted to her only option, a sharp kick against his shins. For the fraction of a second, he dropped his guard.

Tracy realized her move had been an unwise one when he retaliated with such painful pressure on her arms that a tear rolled down her cheeks. Then, with her head still wedged into his chest, she felt the rumble of his voice through his rig cage, the thud of his heartbeat, and heard his terse, icy words zing the air like bullets.

Chapter 14

"So! You've come back to do some more dirty work! Let's see who you are, you tramp!"

His final words were exhaled in a hiss that sent shivers up Tracy's back and reduced her breath to short, shallow gasps. The owner of the rough, menacing voice and the powerful hands holding her captive knew how to use those weapons artfully.

"Let me go!" Tracy's cry was lost in the depths of the villain's sweater. Particles of loose fuzz adhered to her lips and tongue.

Her captor stretched to reach the light switch, loosening his grip on one of Tracy's hands long enough for her to pummel his chest with all the might she could muster. He must not have expected her to have that much fight left, for she felt his muscles tighten and flex. She cringed, expecting retaliation. Just then, his fingers found the switch and the light flicked on.

For a long, incredible moment, they stared at each other until the truth registered and they chorused in unison, "You!"

Tracy was the first to gather her wits. "Why aren't you in bed where you're supposed to be?"

"Me? What about you?" Greg challenged.

"You should know why." Tracy dodged the issue at hand to rework a worn subject. "I've been practically forced to live in this lab since you so brilliantly recommended me for the job while you were gone."

"Some thanks I get!" His attempt to veil a smile angered Tracy even more. "I suggested you because you're one of the few people around here who seem to know what you're doing. I thought you'd appreciate the responsibility. Obviously, I was wrong."

He can be just as bitchy as I can, Tracy thought, as she blazed, "Your heart's about as kindly as a snake's. You might have given me a choice."

"Choice? When the fire began, there wasn't time to beg on bended knee to a high and mighty young lady. I thought you'd have the decency to pitch in and do what was necessary during the emergency. I'm sorry I gave you credit for being above the mob."

That struck Tracy like a stake through the heart, but she could not quit the corner she had weaseled herself into so stubbornly. The words of apology she sought simply would not come without uncorking her true feelings.

"And now," Greg pressed, "please tell me exactly why you're here."

"Because I forgot my log book and I need it tomorrow. Is that so terrible?" To divert his attention from her quivering chin, she added, "How dare you manhandle me!"

Greg slackened his grip, mistaking the tear trickling down her cheek for reaction to pain, not shame, but their bodies remained so closely entwined that an onlooker might have mistaken them for lovers. "How could I know it was you?" Tracy detected a hint of apology in his voice.

"I doubt that my identity would have made one iota of difference to a person with your cavalier attitude, unless you were expecting someone pretty dangerous. Or do you usually treat women like this?"

Still gripping Tracy firmly, Greg narrowed his eyes and said, "Not unless they're up to no good." He paused to consider the situation. "Can you prove you're not the one I'm after?"

Consolidating every furious fiber of her being, Tracy spoke slowly and, she hoped, threateningly. "I don't know who you're after, or why, but if you don't let go of me by the time I count to three, I'll scream so loudly the entire camp will wake up, and I'll tell Doc and everyone how you grabbed me in the dark and hurt me. One … two …"

Greg dropped his hands as suddenly as he had attacked. "Quiet! The last thing I need is a screaming woman."

"No wonder! You're in it so thick not even a crooked lawyer could save you," Tracy said, rubbing her wrists.

"I'm in what? What are you trying to do to me? I go away for a few days thinking I've left my work in the hands of a competent, logical, respectable woman, and come back to this nonsense."

"I will not be used for criminal purposes and I intend to find out why you stole my turquoise. You'd better return it—fast!"

Tracy's words slugged Greg between the eyes. "Your turquoise? Ah ... I see why you're angry, but that's no reason for you to plant that package."

"You're the one who doesn't make sense. I can't imagine what package you're talking about."

"No? Then I suppose you've no idea where this came from?" Greg lunged toward his desk and yanked open the drawer. He drew out the packet the Indian woman had handed Tracy and thrust it under her nose.

"Oh," she managed, in a very small voice. "That completely slipped my mind. It's for Doc."

"For Doc?" He stared at her as if she had gone berserk.

"Yes. An Apache woman brought it."

"What Apache woman?"

"I have no idea who she is. She stopped here this afternoon and dropped it off for Doc. Said he paid her in advance. He was out on the dig, so I put it in the desk for safe keeping. I meant to give it to him before supper, but then you came back from the fire, and I got waylaid in the kitchen, and ... well, everything happened at once."

If Tracy's explanation was simple and logical to her, Greg was not buying it. "My dear young lady, have you the slightest notion what this is?" He placed a lump of dull, reddish-brown stone, covered partially by a layer of milky white, on the palm of his hand and thrust it under her nose.

She pushed his hand away. "It's some sort of rock. Surely you know what it is. After all, you're supposed to be the clever geologist."

His shoulders slumped and his expression softened so quickly she could not tell by the single naked light bulb whether he was about to laugh or cry. Shaking his head, he shoved the packet back into the drawer, then dropped down into the swivel chair and motioned Tracy to take the seat opposite.

She hesitated, not certain whether to stay or prepare for a speedy exit. Tentatively, she propped herself against a chair.

"Sit down properly, Tracy. You're liable to fall. Those legs aren't very secure."

"I really don't have the time to ..."

"You'd better take the time now or be sorry later. No, please don't get upset," this as she tensed. "I'm not going to hurt you again. I'm sorry about what happened, believe me, I am. Just another one of my goofs that doesn't endear me to people. Still, there's good reason why I was so furious. For future reference, there are several things you need to know."

Something in Greg's eyes lowered the barrier that stood between them. Tracy sank slowly into the chair, surprising herself for obeying his command.

His gaze was steady. "You asked why I'm not in bed. That part's easy. With Snakeskin snoring like a chain saw chorus, I couldn't get to sleep, so I decided to come over here to check your work in case I had any questions in the morning before you left for the dig. When I found this package in my desk, I thought you'd left it for me, so I opened it, and when I saw what it is …"

"Well, what *is* it?"

"… I thought someone had planted it to get me in trouble. Since I'm not the most popular guy in camp, I wasn't too surprised, just mad!"

"You still haven't told me."

"You really *don't* know what this is, do you?"

"Greg Delgado, will you please stop treating me as if I'm some sort of criminal! You're the one who should be grilled about the whereabouts of my turquoise. Of course I don't know what that rock is, so will you please tell me and then we can get on to the basic issue of what you plan to do about making good your theft."

"First things first, my sweet."

"Don't you dare 'my sweet' me, you … you …"

A patch of crimson spread across Greg's cheek. "Sorry. Just a figure of speech. No harm intended." He shifted gears quickly back to the cool customer Tracy was beginning to know too well for comfort. "It's fire agate."

She stared blankly. "Fire agate? What's that?"

"You don't know?"

"If I did, would I ask?"

For the first time that evening, he smiled easily. "Well then, you *don't* know."

"Isn't that what I just finished telling you? I suppose you're going to say the stone is illegal."

"Well, yes it is … and no. It depends on the circumstance. We're not allowed to have it in our possession if it was mined here. This is government land, and everything here belongs either to our government or to the Apaches who live here."

"But the woman said it's for Doc. He's already paid her."

"That's the point. If it were a gift, we could let the matter go, but since he paid her for it, it appears that he's not being above board. Even though these are valuable gems, we can't prospect on reservations. Only the Native Americans have that privilege."

Tracy scoffed at the ugly stone. "Gems! That's no gem."

"You'd never think so at first, would you? That shows how well Mother Nature can fool man. When this surface is ground away, the iridescent layers are exposed."

Tracy masked her interest and waited for Greg to continue. He obliged, pulling forth a key chain dangling a green stone. As Tracy studied it closer, an intense light seemed to pulsate from its very core.

"This was given to me by a friend who owns a fire agate mine in the mountains down near Stafford," Greg said. "Since it's on private land, not a reservation, it's perfectly legal."

"It's splendid!" Tracy could not hide her admiration.

"Isn't it! This stone started out exactly like the piece the woman brought today. A lapidary removes the whitish layer and polishes the gem to accent its colors. They're all different. Some are red, brown, and orange, while others are blue, green, and purple. Their unique quality is the fire deep down inside. That distinguishes them from other agates."

Tracy was transfixed by the illusion of a blue flame darting upward from the stone's depths. She had never seen an inanimate object so vibrant. "Are they rare?"

"Rare enough to be classified as a precious gem," Greg said. "No two are alike, and they're practically indestructible because they're so hard nothing can scratch them."

"Sort of like a diamond," Tracy said, ensnared by the spell of the brilliant stone.

"Exactly. Some investors expect them to become as valuable as diamonds one day. That's why people are buying them now to hold until the market grows. It's simply a matter of time." Greg motioned toward the desk drawer. "I suspect this was bought for next to nothing. If the Apaches mined their site systematically and held out for the going price, they might discover that fire agates will increase in value like other desirable natural resources. The gems would be an excellent source of income for them, but they need to be properly monitored to discourage the black market."

"There's a fire agate mine on this reservation?"

He nodded. "Sure is. With the richest deposits ever found, but the Apaches lack the proper equipment and financial backing to get into full production. Right now, the Mexicans have the largest commercial source of fire agates. The stones are found where there's been fairly recent volcanic activity. By that, I'm talking about twenty to forty million years ago."

"These stones are that old?"

"Not quite. They're formed from the volcanic water that seeps into cavities in the earth's surface. As the mineral stays, the agate forms, somewhat like the way a pearl develops in an oyster, and it grows until all the mineral is drained from the volcanic water."

"I imagine that process happens very few places in the world."

"You're right. That makes the few fire agate mines in existence very special. Since the older mines near Mexico City are almost worked out, the jewelers there are looking for good cheap sources. The Apaches on this reservation don't yet understand the commercial value of the gems, so they sell them for a pittance to people here at camp, never suspecting that they'll be passed along to a fence who takes them to Mexico City under the guise of business trips, vacations, or ..."

"Or scientific meetings," Tracy could not help blurting.

Greg grinned broadly. "I knew you'd get the picture."

"Surely you didn't think that I ...?"

"Absolutely not. You were the last one I suspected, until you came creeping in here in the dark."

Tracy bristled. "Creeping! You call that creeping? I walked in and was attacked by a mad man!"

"Now you understand why. We're on government property and I can't stand by while this dig becomes an illegal operation and the Apaches living here are fleeced out of their birthright. I want them to get everything they deserve from their fire agates. Ranching has been their life for years, but there's not enough money in it alone for proper housing, good schools, and the first-rate medical care they deserve."

Tracy was struck by how closely Greg's concerns matched hers. As he talked, she studied his face, trying to sort out her emotions.

"I may not win a popularity contest, but I don't think I deserve having fire agates planted on me," he said. "Agents from the Bureau of Indian Affairs can drop in any time for a spot check. It doesn't happen often, but they come by unannounced to check the camp files and equipment at least once each summer. Unfortunately, they're not authorized to examine personal effects. I'm sure that's where they'd unearth most of the evidence. The minute I found this packet, I knew the problem was greater than I originally thought. I'd just turned out the light and was about to start back to my cabin when I heard your footsteps approaching. I figured that the one responsible might be coming back. Since all the guys are knocked out, I knew it had to be a woman, easy to overpower, so I waited inside the door. The way this package was wrapped, I felt certain it was just the tip of a gem smuggling plot."

"Well I didn't plant it, and you're off the hook, but what about Doc? Why would he be involved?"

"Are you sure she said it was for Doc?" Greg's dark eyes pierced hers.

"I'm positive." As Tracy stared back at him, something clicked. "At least I *think* that's who she meant. You don't suppose …?"

"Now you're plugged in. You were about to say …?"

"Woody. Why else would he leave the comforts of home to come here?"

"That bothers you, too?"

"Yes … but so much doesn't make sense. A successful doctor wouldn't dabble in illegal ventures and risk his reputation. Would he?"

"Why not? He has the opportunity for a profit now, or a bonanza later on when the gems soar in value. They've tripled in just the past five years."

Tracy frowned. "Still, how can Woody get away with it?"

"Probably because physicians are respected by everyone and they have the wherewithal to vacation in Mexico City, Acapulco, or the Yucatan peninsula. If he goes about it one trip at a time, year after year, he'd have to make an awfully big slip to attract the attention of the authorities. He's not the type of person to be arrested merely on suspicion. We need proof."

"We? You and who else? How do you know so much about him?"

Greg leaned forward and lowered his voice. "The BIA suspected that gems were being smuggled out of here two summers ago. Because I'm a geologist with a university connection and can become part of the project without arousing suspicion, they asked me to monitor the situation. I caught several students taking a few low quality stones last summer and Doc agreed to dismiss them, but when the loss increased after their departure and the blame leaned toward Woody, Doc refused to take any action against his old buddy."

"Friendship's a funny thing," Tracy mused.

"Sometimes it's as blind as love." Greg tossed her a sideways glance. "The damage will come if Woody is finally tagged and it reflects on Doc's integrity. He'll be blamed, too, and maybe even pressured to close the field school."

"So you're a vigilante committee of one."

He nodded. "By default."

Tracy shook a finger in his face. "What you've told me is very interesting, but you still haven't explained why you removed my turquoise from the materials going to the museum. You even struck out all reference to it in the notes."

"You're a top notch detective, Tracy, but now you're putting me on the spot. I'd hoped I wouldn't have to get into a distasteful subject, but I owe it to you." Greg expelled a long breath. "I gather that you're pretty fond of Doc. At least you accepted the job at the university and you seem to get along well with him."

"I can't imagine anyone not getting along with Doc. He so jolly and kind. You don't often meet a famous person with such an outgoing personality. But what does that have to do with …?"

"Everything. I'm just as fond of Doc as you are. I've known him most of my life and he's been—almost like a father to me. I guess you know that I work for an oil company helping them explore and develop new resources, but I started out planning to go into anthropology, simply because I idolized Doc. The more I observed the academic world, the faster I became convinced that it's too conniving for me. I'm not very subtle, and I'm completely out of it when it comes to faculty rivalry between professors who think they have to publish or perish. In Doc's case, he's always felt the pressure to make a 'remarkable discovery.'"

"Doc doesn't have to worry. He's made so many great discoveries that he's miles ahead of his colleagues."

Greg raised his eyebrows. "You believe he can keep that up indefinitely?"

"Judging by his accomplishments, I should think so. I'm always running across his articles in scientific journals. Every time he goes out into the field, he adds to our knowledge about early civilizations. He and his students are always digging up something significant. I was thrilled about coming to Juniper Junction because it's been such a rich site." Tracy paused to evaluate Greg's expression. "Why do you have that sarcastic look on your face? You were right there when I found the turquoise."

"Yes, I was there. He could have fooled me, too, if I hadn't known better."

"What do you mean?" Tracy fairly shouted. "The bracelet was in the bowl. It was buried in soil and never saw the light of day until I dug it out."

"That's what they said about the Piltdown Man. The soil around him had been disturbed and replaced without anyone becoming the wiser. Doc does some of his best reconstruction during the wee morning hours."

Tracy knew full well the story of the British scientist who planted a curious skull in an unlikely layer of earth just to trick the experts. "Surely you're not saying that Doc has pulled off a hoax!"

"Remember, Tracy, it took years of research before men who should have known better were able to prove that they'd been had."

She studied Greg's expression, that inexplicable twist of the mouth and those deep, unfathomable eyes. Was he hiding something? The suggestion that Doc Baxter had deceived the international fellowship of anthropologists and unwittingly jeopardized his own career was too improbable. She had listened to Greg out of curiosity, if not out of fear for her own being, but now she was unable to shake the feeling that he was lying to save his own face. Evenly, she said, "I'm afraid I don't believe one word you're saying about Doc. He *never* would sacrifice his integrity to plant a bracelet, or anything else, just to make a name for himself."

"That's what I told myself the first time I caught him seeding the ground," Greg said. "He does it all the time, you know, projectile points popping up everywhere, like magic. It took me a long time to accept this weakness and remind myself that he has more virtues than a lot of men."

"You're saying this isn't the first time?"

"I'm afraid not. I found him out about six years ago, but it probably goes back much earlier. I've tried to keep him above reproach by removing questionable artifacts from the shipments we send to the university museum. It takes so many years for the staff to get around to cataloguing each shipment that nobody there would know if something had been left out, or if there were reason to suspect a fraud."

"But that bracelet didn't come out of the blue. If it's not a relic, then it was made recently. Supposing Doc commissioned someone to make my bracelet? If so, the artisan would have to be a Native American, most likely one on this reservation."

"I can't be certain, but everything points there. He's on friendly terms with them, they can always use extra money, and they know how to keep secrets."

"And Diane's turquoise? That's a fake, too?"

"The turquoise is real enough, just a rough chunk, no attempt to put it into a setting. From what I saw, it was one of Doc's more amateurish jobs, a hurry-up affair to give some kind of back-up credibility to your find."

"Snakeskin seemed to think it passed muster," Tracy said.

"No reason for him to think otherwise. When a man has a reputation in the field as firm as Doc's, people look upon events that are out of the ordinary as holy miracles rather than everyday fraud."

Tracy felt her blood rising, but she was more angry with her own disbelief than with Greg. He was defaming a man admired and honored by scholars in his field the world over, a man who had been kind enough to hire her as his assistant, for whatever reason, she did not care.

She wanted to reject Greg's premise for the simple reason that she could not believe ill of Doc. The longer she mulled over her situation, the more she resented Greg manipulating her thoughts as if he were a psychologist programming an unsuspecting rat to gobble up bait. Defiantly, she opened her mouth to call his bluff, but at that moment he reached into a low drawer, drew out a box, and pressed it into her palm.

"Here's your turquoise bracelet, Tracy," he said. "Believe me, it's a genuine piece of art work by a Twentieth Century human. Go ahead. Take it. You're welcome to have it examined and appraised by an expert of your choice."

Tracy felt the blood rise in her face as she toyed with the box. Greg rose from his chair, more like a sleek cougar on the prowl than a man fighting sleep. He regarded her solemnly, perhaps waiting for a perfunctory thanks. She nodded imperceptibly, unable to speak through the choking sensation in her throat, caring not in the least how Greg took her response, and darted past him out the door.

Without looking back, she sensed the lab light being doused, heard the door close quietly and the shuffle of Greg's boots across the porch and down the steps. Tracy fought back tears as she fled to her cabin, mindful of the swaying pines, their branches worried by the cold wind sweeping across the plateau.

Many an eerie tale was inspired by a night such as this, she reflected, a night fit for little but toppling the heads of sinister horsemen or rattling the bones of disinterred skeletons.

Chapter 15

By breakfast, Bill had regained his braggadocio. He caught up with Tracy on the way into the dining room, full of smiles and remorse for having ignored her after dinner.

"The truth is, we worked so hard at the fire we had trouble keeping awake when we got back," he said. "I promise to be livelier this evening, so be sure to save me a seat at the sing-along after Doc's lecture."

Tracy looked askance at him. "That's twelve hours away. Anything could happen. I might even be stuck in the lab afterward."

Bill settled himself across the table from her. "You wouldn't be trying to give me the brush-off?"

Marie, overhearing, slid onto the bench next to Tracy and gave her a healthy nudge. "Why would she to that? All women welcome a hero's attention."

Outwardly, Bill let Marie's taunt roll over him like so much maple syrup, but Tracy knew by the way he mulled over his coffee that the sarcasm had hit its mark. Even when the rest were trying to put the day's schedule in focus, Bill usually chattered non-stop at breakfast. If he suspected that Tracy knew the less popular version of his behavior at the forest fire, he had chosen to tough it out, hoping she would discount anything she might have heard.

Marie was about to drain the pitcher of orange juice when she looked up and saw Ray coming through the door. "I was wondering if you'd make it," she said, smiling broadly. "All caught up on your sleep, honey?"

Ray shook his head. "Not by a mile. I've been listening on the radio to the guys over at Gila Peak. They seem to have the fire under control, but even if they don't put it out completely, the rains will finish the job in a day or so."

Bill perked up. "So the monsoons are coming, are they?"

Ray shot him a disparaging glance. "They usually do about this time. You should know that."

"It would have to be a heavy rain to drown a forest fire," Tracy said.

Bill laughed. "Heavy! That's hardly the word. It comes in torrents. When the dry arroyos flood, it's Niagara Falls in the desert."

"That's the truth," Marie said. "Even more amazing, the next day you'd never know it passed through."

Tracy turned to Ray. "How do the rains affect the dig?"

"Everything stops until the sun comes out," Ray said. "If you cover your materials with canvas, no harm is done. There'll be thick clouds, thunder, lightning, the usual warning signs."

"Then there's nothing to worry about." Tracy downed another spoonful of oatmeal.

"Not if it doesn't hold up our work," Marie said. "Honestly though, I'm so exhausted from digging that I'd welcome a reprieve." She speared a waffle from the platter making the rounds.

"If you keep eating like that, you'll need all the work you can get to hold your weight down," Ray warned, grinning. "You won't be so cute when you're fat and forty."

"Hush your fuss," Marie said. "The way I'm slaving, I'm more apt to be a bag of bones by the end of the summer."

"And then there's Tracy, who's exactly right," Bill said.

"Flattery will get you nowhere," Tracy said.

"Not even a seat next to you tonight?"

Tracy began to wonder if she was being too harsh and reserved. Relenting, she said, "Maybe. If you promise not to pester me again."

"Promise. Not for another twenty-four hours."

Tracy could not help laughing at the solemn expression he contrived.

As the crew rode out to the dig in the back of the stake truck, she became mindful of pink streaks across the eastern sky that might have been daubed by a celestial hand dipping into a giant paint bucket. The magnificent expanse gave no hint of the storm Ray predicted.

After dropping off the broadside crew, Snakeskin drove Tracy and Becky to a virgin site at the farthest end of the plateau. Novice that she was, Tracy saw nothing on the surface worth investigating, but if Doc's divining powers were accurate, she felt confidant they would strike something farther down.

Snakeskin idled the engine only long enough for the two to jump off the truck and cast out their tools and the lunches Clarence had packed. Eager to find new treasures, they scooped away the top layer of soil even before the dust churned up by the departing truck had settled.

As Tracy and Becky exposed each layer, they alternately sacked the debris and wiped perspiration trickling from their brows. The powdery dirt streaking their faces was quickly transformed into damp globules of mud, reminding Tracy of war paint.

As the morning dragged on, oppressive heat began settling around them like an unwelcome mongrel. On previous days, dry air and strong winds made the atmosphere refreshing, but this day was different. As the humidity built, Tracy's limbs became heavy and her head throbbed. The more water she swigged from her canteen, the thirstier she felt. She wished she could crawl into a dark hole, but their excavation was too shallow, and there was no visible shelter nearby. She even began to regret her campaign to defy Greg. The paper work and puzzle pieces that had confronted her in the lab were beginning to look far more tempting than death by dehydration.

Because Tracy and Becky were working so far from camp, Doc had decided they would stay at the site all day. The Forestdale crew had followed that routine and never complained about losing a long lunch break, but this new situation helped Tracy realize how fortunate the broadside workers had been to have their noon meal in the cool shelter of the stone dining hall. The open plain, she realized, was no substitute for the rustic comforts of camp.

Her cheese sandwich was limp, the apple was as hot as pie filling straight from the oven, and the melted chocolate chips puddled beneath the cookie dough in the waxed paper wrapping. As sporadic winds blew dirt from the excavation over the food spread before them, Tracy lost her appetite. She wadded the sandwich and cookies into their wrappings and sat them aside. Becky was less selective. She consumed her lunch with cheerful resignation, blowing grains of dust from her sandwich and licking the chocolate puddles. When every morsel was gone, she lay back and closed her eyes while Tracy made entries in their log.

"You're very easy to please," Tracy said.

"I've had worse, much worse," Becky said.

"I believe you'd survive even if civilization as we know it were totally wiped out." Tracy smiled to herself, remembering how stoically Becky had managed without her trunk for the first few weeks.

"I'd soldier on," Becky said. "Never could figure out why people need a lot of possessions. They tie you down. I like to travel loose, like the tribes who lived on the plains. They survived for generation after generation with only what nature gave them. They gathered food from the ground or caught it on the run. The tribes who lived at Juniper Junction built homes of soil and stones, and made their pottery from clay, all natural materials, not lousy plastics that don't self-destruct. When I die, I plan to be buried in the elements. No gaudy casket for me. Maybe a nice, simple burial at sea, or cremation with my ashes scattered over the mountains. Something easy to engineer ... and easy to forget."

"Your family might have other ideas," Tracy said.

"They don't care, I'm sure. Too busy being successful and social. We pretty much go our separate ways. My tuition is paid automatically from a trust fund. I manage quite nicely on next to nothing."

"You never see your family?"

"Nope." Becky chewed lazily on a stalk of prairie grass. "I don't think they'd want me cluttering up their neighborhood. It's terribly posh, you know. They're happy telling friends that I'm away at a high profile college. Besides, I'm happiest when I'm alone and not expected to conform to their ways. Oh bother! The sun's going in. Must be getting late. We'd better finish what we can before Snakeskin comes back."

Tracy glanced skyward. Becky was right about the sun. For the first time since their arrival at Juniper Junction, it was blocked by black clouds congealing into a low, threatening canopy. These were the rain clouds revered for centuries by the people who inhabited the land, subjects of prayers, objects of worship, and depicted by artisans on pottery, jewelry, masks, Kachina dolls, and garments to ward off danger.

For Tracy, the sight of a rain cloud obscuring the sun was as common as a pigeon strutting down Fifth Avenue, but to the Southwest Indians, it heralded a personal communication from the gods. Had she understood the monsoons, she would have been more respectful of their power; instead, she anticipated a minor inconvenience, nothing more.

The first lightning bolt tore through the clouds at mid-afternoon, a jagged red poker touching down west of the camp. In its wake, a clap of thunder reverberated through the ground. The sky grew dark, but no rain fell even though the lightning flashed and sizzled wantonly. With each stroke, its partner roll of thunder rumbled closer.

By the time winds dislodged the large rocks Tracy had positioned at every corner of the excavation and shredded the canvas, she abandoned trying to protect the excavation and their materials. Alarmed, she shouted above the wind, "Becky! We're too exposed here. We should lie down flat."

"Looks like a low spot up ahead," Becky called back. "Let's go!"

Heads bent, they ran close to the ground until they reached the rim of a gully.

Tracy hesitated. "Are you sure we should jump down there?"

"It's the safest place to be," Becky said, with authority. "I know that much. The rule on the golf course is to find the lowest spot and avoid standing near trees."

While Tracy was still pondering the wisdom of seeking shelter in a depression, the lightning and thunder merged into a solitary boom that sent them sprawling. At that instant, the clouds opened. Without further discussion, they leaped into the ditch.

Pelted by the merciless downpour, Tracy and Becky hovered together. Minutes passed. As the water began rising over their boots, the reality of their situation became apparent. They were between two dangers: a dry creek bed fast becoming a conduit for water streaming off the mountains, and the electric jolts ricocheting off higher ground.

"I may have made a mistake," Becky said. "Maybe good sense on the golf course doesn't apply to our situation."

"That's exactly what I was thinking," Tracy said. The curtain of water gushing from the heavens was so intense that she could not see the opposite bank clearly. Drenched and terrified, she huddled against the wall of dirt that was fast turning into cascading slime. Thick chunks broke away from the bank and splashed into the swirl of mud lapping their ankles.

"If this keeps up much longer, there'll be nothing left of our excavation," Becky said.

"Or our logs," Tracy said. "Even if the notebooks aren't washed away, the pages will be soaked."

Becky glanced down at her feet. "The water's almost to the top of our boots. I think the time has come to make a quick exit from this trench. Come on, Tracy."

Another bolt of lightning zigzagged across the plains, followed almost instantly by a deafening thunder clap. Tracy hesitated. "Are you sure we won't put ourselves in a worse fix? The lightning scares me."

"Which is worse, death by drowning or being fried to a crisp?" Not waiting for an answer, Becky heaved herself out of the excavation and onto the ground, then rolled out of sight.

Tracy wanted to follow suit, but even as she vacillated between remaining or taking her chance on the open range, she became aware of an oncoming roar, like a mighty locomotive high-balling down the rails. At first, she judged it to be the sound of the wind, but the tone was far more ominous, deeper and utterly unyielding. At the precise moment she heard a warning cry borne by the winds, like someone calling her name, invisible flood gates parted directly ahead sending a wall of water rushing toward her.

It hit like a bomb, knocking Tracy off her feet and sucking her beneath the surface. She felt her body scrape against rocks, dragged against her will, her head pounding and her lungs about to burst. Another surge sent her tumbling head over heels. Instinctively, her arms flailed to lessen the impact of her collision with the bank. The force of the onrushing water buffeted her against the side once, twice. The third time she crashed against the bank, a sharp object dug into her side, tearing her flesh, ripping her shirt, and halting her momentum. As the water swept past, she realized that she was being held by a few strands of cloth impaled on an exposed tree root. She clung to her life-saver tenaciously, defying the swirling waters that sought to dislodge her hold.

"Help!" She screamed before filthy liquid rushed into her mouth and nose. Spewing it out, she screamed again, "Becky!"

The only reply was the roaring current sluicing through the gully. When she heard her name shouted again, she thought it was a trick of the mind. Seconds later, a powerful hand clutched her wrist and a voice ordered, "Hold on, Tracy. Here! Give me your other hand."

She looked up into Greg's face. He was lying prone on the ground, his arms stretched toward her. Inexplicably, she began fighting his rescue attempt. What, she wondered, had overcome her common sense? Was she trying to punish him for discrediting Doc in her eyes? Near delirium, she allowed petulance to overwhelm her and deny him the satisfaction of pulling her to safety until he met her demand. "You have to get Becky first."

"Cut the nonsense!" Greg tugged at Tracy's arm until she thought he would wrench it from its socket. "Help me, Tracy. You're like a dead weight. Your boots are filled with water. Kick them off so I can pull you out."

At that moment, she panicked, realizing that she no longer had the edge. "I … I can't The laces are knotted."

Greg swore beneath his breath. "Then grab onto my arm and try to hoist yourself up. I'll steady you."

Tracy struggled, but gained no ground. Gasping, she said, "I can't. Get Becky first, then I'll catch my breath and try again."

"Becky's safe. You're the problem. Now push!"

"What do you mean she's safe?"

"Just that. Try to put your arms around my neck ... now hold on tight."

Succumbing to Greg's powerful muscles and willpower, Tracy allowed him to haul her onto the ground. As she burst into hot tears, he yanked her to her feet and began pulling her toward his truck parked higher on the track.

Seeing no sign of Becky, Tracy panicked once more. "You lied to me, Greg. Becky's gone." Without provocation, she began beating his chest and screaming, "Becky! Becky! Don't let her die!"

Greg tolerated the barrage of her fists without flinching, but Tracy saw his jaw tighten and the veins on his temple bulge. She continued pounding him, her voice growing more hoarse with each sob, until he looked directly at her, his eyes blazing, his voice steady and low. "Stop it right now, Tracy."

With that, he hoisted her off the ground, ignoring her whimpers, and set out once more for the truck.

She had steeled herself for bad news about Becky, but once Greg propped her upright and opened the door to reach for a blanket, she could not believe her eyes.

"Hi, Tracy." Becky sat there, huddled in a blanket. "I was sure Greg could save you."

"How ... how did you get here?"

"Greg found me and brought me to his truck."

"Becky was making pretty good progress up the hill by the time I came along," Greg said, as he wrapped the blanket around Tracy. "Now hold still while I help you into the truck."

Thoroughly swaddled, her energy drained, Tracy said nothing as Greg lifted her onto the seat next to Becky. By the time he jumped into the driver's seat and switched on the engine and heater, she was filled with remorse and shivering from the cold.

"You two may not realize it, but you're lucky to be alive," Greg said. "You weren't prepared to expect this kind of storm, let alone survive it."

"I've never been in anything like that flood," Becky said. "It came out of nowhere."

"If you were natives of the Southwest, you would have learned about the danger of arroyos before you began to walk," Greg said.

"Arroyos?"

"That's Spanish for dry creek beds. They look perfectly innocent most of the year, but they turn into killers when the monsoons come. Rivers and creeks can't hold the water. Anything caught in the current is swept away. The force is so great I've seen oil tankers and houses carried downstream for a half mile or more."

"Then human beings wouldn't have a chance," Becky said.

"Not likely," Greg said. "It takes some mighty fervent prayers to escape that kind of power."

"You must have prayed a lot for the strength to save us." Becky's voice was filled with admiration.

"Every inch of the way," Greg said.

Tracy, huddled in the blanket, was gripped by shame. She knew that her behavior toward Greg had been petulant and completely out of character. She fervently wished she could take back her hateful words. While Greg and Becky chatted, the windshield wipers seemed to chant, "You're safe, you're safe, you're safe." She was still trying to formulate an apology when Becky poked her with an elbow.

"Did my eyes deceive me, Tracy? I could have sworn I saw you giving Greg a going over. That's not exactly the way to treat a rescuer."

Greg cast an impish smile in Tracy's direction. "You weren't deceived, Becky. I'm her favorite punching bag. We'll excuse her because she was thinking of you instead of herself." Growing more serious, he added, "In times of danger, people often become illogical. They substitute anger at another person instead of coming to grips with their own fears."

"That's easy to understand," Becky said. "All the while I was scrambling away from the flood, I was venting my fury at Doc for leaving us out there all day."

"My thoughts exactly," Greg said. "That was an unwise decision on his part, especially when he knows the danger of storms like this. I would have come after you sooner, but he didn't explain your situation to me until the rain had already begun. I drove as fast as I could, and by the time I found you, I knew it would be touch and go rescuing Tracy. She wasn't the easiest load I ever hauled. Those sopping wet jeans and boots filled with water added quite a few pounds." He laughed lightly. "I exhausted so much energy lugging her back to the truck that I had to conserve strength by not talking, so I never did explain how I knew you were safe before she began her barrage."

"Oh," Tracy said, too ashamed to look his way. She remained silent for the rest of the drive.

As the truck pulled alongside the lab, Doc rushed out. "Good job, Greg! It's a miracle you got them. If I'd realized how bad the storm would be, we would have had them out of there early."

Even before Greg lifted Tracy from the truck and extracted her from the swaddling blanket, Brenda had reached Becky from the driver's side and hustled her into the lab.

Doc lingered alongside until Tracy was standing on her own. Giving her a fatherly hug, he said, "You owe your life to Greg. I know you've thanked him a thousand times over."

Tracy bit her lip, too mortified to admit that Doc credited her with an undeserved kindness.

Greg patted Tracy's shoulder. "She's upset, and no wonder. It was bad."

Tracy searched his face, grateful that he had not betrayed her. She was about to express her gratitude, when Bill stepped from the sea of faces, threw his arms around her, and began kissing her.

"Stop it!" She strained to push him away. "I don't need your smothering. All I want is a hot shower and dry clothes."

Over Bill's shoulder, Tracy saw Greg wheel about and set off purposely toward the bath house, waving away questions from Stu and Joe who bounded off the porch after him.

Even as she watched Greg disappear down the path, the storm began to ebb as quickly as it had begun, the sheets of water pouring just moments before from the lab's tin roof dwindling to infrequent drops, a signal for those still on the porch to rush down the steps and gather around Tracy. Iris, sensing Tracy's dilemma, pushed through the knot of bodies and wrenched her arm free of Bill's grasp.

"Gangway, everyone," Iris ordered. "Questions later. I'm going to make sure she doesn't get pneumonia."

Like a mother hen, Iris steered Tracy through the group and down the path to the bath house. High above, suspended between the pueblo and the farthest ridge, a rainbow materialized.

Chapter 16

By morning, the sun was ablaze, the birds were chirping, and there was scant physical evidence at camp of the deluge, except for clumps of dead tree branches and piles of pine cones washed from higher elevations. Bursting with his usual optimism, Doc assured Tracy and Becky that it was safe to return to their strat test. They were skeptical at first of his promise that the arroyo would be empty and back to normal, but when they reached the site, they found no signs of water damage other than piles of stones and debris newly deposited alongside. Even the excavation was clear, no matter that the wind had whisked away the tarp. Except for damp soil near the bottom layers, little had changed. They set to work immediately.

Their shovels penetrated deep into the softened mass, allowing the task to go faster than before. Tracy's muscles labored intently to complete the chore; all the while, her mind replayed the events of the previous day, immune to Becky's incessant chatter. Only Doc's arrival forced a truce in the mental battle that pitted her sense of honor against superficial pride.

After perusing their accomplishments at the site, Doc lingered, ostensibly to discuss the role he expected her to play on campus come fall. He was at his charming best, all the more reason Tracy resolved to confine their relationship to the business arrangement it warranted. Despite the lines creasing his brow and the silver streaking his black hair at the temples, he was uncommonly handsome, a magnet for women of every age. As she studied him in the bright sunlight, she was overcome by a hollow feeling in the pit of her stomach. For the first time, she acknowledged that his respected reputation as a scholar probably came at the expense of honesty.

As they talked, Tracy wondered if he knew what she knew about the turquoise incident. His implication in the deceit was not apparent in his hooded eyes. Each time he heaped praise upon her for the discovery he had plotted, she parried his words and diverted him to another topic. Until she collected more evidence, it was imperative that she delay the inevitable confrontation.

While Tracy sifted through clods of soil that Becky flipped onto the screen, Doc poked around the trash pile, picking up projectile points and bits of obsidian that she could have sworn were not there before he arrived. At length, he leaned over and spoke quietly to her, excluding Becky from the conversation. "As soon as you finish here, I'd like to shift you to a real bonanza, something to cap the summer in the best way possible."

Tracy eyed him warily. "What do you have in mind?"

"I have a hunch. Right next to the pueblo, there's another spot that bears investigation. In view of the turquoise you found, I'm betting we'll find even more in this location."

Tracy, now certain he was plotting to seed another site, had no intention of playing the dupe. "That's a tall order. Why don't you save it until next year? It would be something special to look forward to."

He thought that over before flashing a mechanical smile. "Maybe you're right. Perhaps we don't have enough time this summer to do it justice." He clapped his hands to indicate a subject change. "Well now, I don't mean to hold you up. Snakeskin will come to get you in a little while. Or maybe it's Greg. I forget who's scheduled to make the rounds today. Does it make any difference to you?"

"Of course not. Why should it?"

Tracy sensed that Doc was studying her expression with more than casual interest. "I get the impression that you resent Greg. Any reason why you two don't get along?"

"You jump to conclusions. There's no basis for thinking that I resent Greg. In fact, I'm very grateful to him for rescuing us."

"Good, good. Even though this is his last season with us, I'll expect him to stop around at my office whenever he's in town …"

Tracy, catching the drift of his thinking, cut in, "And you're telling me this because you don't want any friction. Don't worry. I respect his expertise and honesty."

Satisfied, Doc returned to his truck and Tracy expelled a sigh of relief. She had never bargained for a chance to bore into the soul of a great man. To her dismay, she was becoming uneasy in his presence.

For the next few days, Bill hovered solicitously near, giving Tracy further reason to feel uncomfortable. Her doubts about him persisted right up to the afternoon the trucks arrived at camp simultaneously. They pulled in within a few yards of the strange Jeep parked by the office.

The girl perched on the fender would have been a show-stopper in any setting, but her skin-tight toreador pants and slinky satin top were downright irreverent at camp. An unexpected chill fanned the silent exodus from the trucks. Except for several furtive nods, Tracy initially had no indication that anyone recognized the newcomer. Moment later, their brisk scattering *en masse* to the cabins was sufficient proof that the girl was no stranger. Left alone on the driveway with Bill, she watched, transfixed, while the girl slithered down from her seat in slow motion, tossed her abundant hair, and confronted them, a smirk scrawled across her classic features.

"You always manage to find the pretty ones, darling," she said. "Have you told her about … *us*?"

If Bill was startled, he never let on. "Funny, funny, my love. You haven't lost your sense of humor. And you look spectacular, doesn't she, Tracy?"

Tracy was too stunned to speak.

The newcomer did not suffer the same reaction. "So! Your name's Tracy. Mine's Tish … Tish Blackman at present, but it'll be Tish Harrison after Bill and I are married in September." She gazed insolently at Tracy, never extinguishing the sultry smile.

Tracy's shock turned to anger as fast as Tish's manufactured eyelashes blinked. "Of course. You're Bill's fiancée, that's easy to see. He's a lucky man to have such a beautiful, devoted girl waiting at home."

Tracy could not see Bill's face, but she sensed his body sag imperceptibly next to her. Was it relief or embarrassment? Tish's eyes darted back and forth from Bill to Tracy, waiting to trap one of them in a lie. Failing that, she dropped her ploy and said, "I see I've misjudged you, Bill. Ever the faithful sweetheart, eh?"

He laughed, relieved. "What else would you expect?"

Before Tish could spit out a litany of expectations, Tracy said, "You two deserve each other, it's obvious, so if you'll excuse me …" She departed with a flourish, hoping that her over-the-shoulder glance at Bill was sufficiently withering.

She had no idea what Tish and Bill would say to each other, but she knew what she would say to those who claiming to be her friends. Bursting into her cabin, she confronted Diane, stretched out on her cot, as usual, idly filing her nails. "Why didn't somebody tell me that Bill is engaged?"

Diane glanced up, mildly surprised. "I thought you knew."

"How could I possibly know?"

"He didn't tell you?"

"Of course not."

"I should have guessed. That's his usual tack. Leads them on until the end of summer. Then he crawls back to Tish and lets her support him during the school year."

"And she goes along with it?"

"Apparently so. He has a roving eye and she has a great business—owns a very ritzy furniture shop in town—so they go their separate ways in the summer. While he's up here romancing the lady most likely, she's at home dating her buyers. So I'm told. Now that's he's getting out of grad school, I'm not surprised they've finally set the date."

Tracy flopped down on her cot. "He's an absolute cad!"

"Gee, Tracy, if I'd known you'd take it so hard, I would've warned you. I thought coming from New York you'd be more sophisticated about men."

"I'm not taking it hard. I simply resent being used, and I'm furious that none of you told me the truth. Everyone kept encouraging me, even though I really didn't care all that much for him from day one. Not even Doc told me!"

Diane rolled over to paw through her toiletries for the right shade of nail polish. "Doc never interferes in the private lives of his students or staff."

Until the dinner gong sounded, Tracy brooded over what she would say to Bill the next time they were alone together. Once in the dining hall, her innate restraint leaped to the fore and she managed to remain cheerful and talkative throughout dinner, oblivious to the undercurrent about Tish and her visit timed to knock the roving pins from under Bill.

Tish remained at camp for the weekend, leaving after Sunday dinner. Tracy had no trouble staying out of her way. There were the endless lab chores, technical books in the library to study, and notes to put in order. If anyone believed that Tracy was pining away because of Bill, they were mistaken. With no ties of the heart looming to deter her from work, she crossed off countless pesky chores by the time the final "lights out" gong sounded Sunday evening.

Closing the door of the lab behind her, she stepped onto the porch. During the evening, the strains of singing had drifted into the lab. Tracy had planned to join the others gathered around the campfire to sing along with Snakeskin as he strummed ballads on his guitar, but by the time she finished her tasks,

Snakeskin had reached the end of his repertoire and some of the group began moving away. Most were heading for a solid night's rest to prepare for work the next morning. Several couples sauntered off through the trees.

For some time, Tracy gazed at the sky. As she inhaled the cool, fresh air that rippled the pines ever so gently, a calm strength surged through her body and she resolved to fulfill some long overdue obligations first thing in the morning. She had just started toward her cabin when a figure stepped from the shadows and grabbed her arm.

"Bill! What do you think you're doing?"

"Taking up where we left off before we were so rudely interrupted," he said.

Tracy wrenched her arm from his grasp. "You are either woefully stupid or vicious!"

"No sweat, sweetheart. Tish has gone. We're all alone. Just you and me for the rest of the summer."

Tracy drew herself up to her full height. "Now I know you're a fool! Otherwise there's no way you could possibly believe I'd have anything to do with you under the circumstances. To be truthful, I never cared much for you anyway."

Bill chuckled. "You're just saying that because you're wild about me."

Tracy stamped her foot. "Will you get this through your thick skull once and for all: I do not now, and never will, think of you as anything but a big-mouthed louse. What kind of person are you to chase after other women behind your fiancée's back? And what kind of person do you think I am? I have no intention of being anyone's second-hand romance!"

"Tracy, you're way behind the times. Everyone's doing it. What harm is there in some extra-curricular romance? Life's for kicks."

Slowly and evenly, Tracy said, "You dare to come one step closer and you'll get a *real* kick out of life. If these boots make hard contact with your anatomy, perhaps *then* you'll understand that some women don't fall for your Don Juan methods."

Whatever Bill was about to say blurred into an embarrassed laugh.

Tracy shook her fist at him. "Well ... don't just stand there! Get moving right out of my life! You're blocking my view of the sky."

"As you wish, milady." He slipped quickly into the trees, his footsteps masked by the pine carpet.

Tracy sank down on the circular bench surrounding the great pine tree and muttered to herself, "The nerve of him! The absolute nerve!"

A voice from the darkness said, "Bravo, Tracy! That's telling him off."

Tracy leaped from her seat and ran toward her unseen audience sitting in the shadows on the far side. At the moment of recognition, she gasped aloud. "You! What are you doing here? How dare you eavesdrop on me!"

Chapter 17

Greg raised his hand defensively. "Please don't start on me again, Tracy. Experiencing your wrath is like being on the business end of a battering ram."

She was about to launch into a tongue lashing when the suppressed chuckle in Greg's voice arrested the temper surging within her. Tracy dissolved into laughter. When at last she caught her breath, she confessed, "If I'd known we had an audience, I might not have had the nerve to say some of the things I said."

"And I never would have sat down here if I'd expected to be at the center of a scene from a soap opera," Greg said.

"Why didn't you let us know you were here?"

"It seemed more prudent to keep quiet and hope you didn't notice me."

"You made a very wise decision." Tracy dropped down beside him. "I think Bill gets the message. Still, I don't understand why nobody told me about him"

"People don't want to get involved."

"That's your excuse?"

"Considering how ballistic you can get when I'm around, I was certain you wouldn't believe me if I told you there was another woman in the picture."

"I hate to admit my failings, but you're probably right. It would have seemed as unreal as the turquoise story." She touched his sleeve. "I'm so sorry I didn't believe you at first, Greg. I do now."

"Oh?" Even in the dark, Tracy detected his grin. "Does that mean we're finally on friendly terms?"

"Of course we are. I've been the one at fault. To tell the truth, I've been afraid of you since that night in the elevator."

He laughed aloud. "So that's what set you off! You must have thought I was being fresh and trying to pick you up. Why didn't you give me a chance to introduce myself and explain that I was on my way to Juniper Junction?"

"When it comes to strange men, I run first and ask questions later," she said. "I should have adhered to that policy when people started pushing Bill at me without filling in the vital details."

"That's worried me all along," Greg said. "I was afraid you had something going with that character, but tonight's performance makes me feel better. You did yourself proud."

"Thanks." Tracy's eyes had adjusted to the dark enough so she could see Greg's profile. He seemed to be studying the sky. "And Greg ..."

"Hmmmm?"

'Thank you, for something else."

His head turned slightly. "For what?"

"As if you didn't know. For saving my life."

"Oh, that. My pleasure."

"I'm ashamed I was so childish. I'm sorry I said what I did, and ..."

"Hush! No apologies necessary. Think about the future, Tracy. It's going to be fine." He pointed to the heavens. "See, what did I tell you? Look up there!"

Tracy held her breath as a star streaked obliquely across the blackness. "Oh Greg! It's beautiful!"

"Quick now, make a wish."

"A wish? Does it work?"

"Always. Falling stars never fail."

Tracy closed her eyes and wished fervently. "There! I've done it! Did you make a wish too?"

"Indeed I did."

"Then both of our wishes should come true." Tracy settled back against the tree and let her eyes sweep the sky from horizon to horizon. "Was that really a falling star?"

"If you want to be technical, no," Greg said. "I didn't want to ruin your illusion. Actually, it probably was an asteroid, what's left of a planet that tried to form between Earth and Mars. The conditions weren't right, so it became a massive trash pile. Every so often, particles of debris break loose from their orbit and plunge into the atmosphere. They've been putting on a pretty good show for centuries, enough to make people around the world sit up and take notice. At times, men have believed they were omens from the heavens. The more romantic viewers decided they were worth wishing on. I'm inclined to go along with them."

"Do the stars—asteroids—fall often?"

"If the sky's clear and you know where to look, you can see them just about every evening. There've been nights when I've seen dozens within minutes, especially this time of year."

"Wow! You must have had a lot of wishes come true."

Greg laughed softly. "In the long run, there's only one wish that counts and I'm still waiting for the answer."

"What do you wish for?"

"Now, Tracy. You should know better than to ask. If I told, it wouldn't come true."

"When it does, will you let me know?"

He considered her question, then nodded. "It's a deal. As soon as Orion slays the Great Bear."

She sat up. "What are you talking about?"

"An old Indian legend, Tracy. Look up there." He pointed to a bright row of stars. "That's Orion's belt. He was a fierce hunter who stalked the Great Bear. The Great Bear is right over there," he said, indicating another segment of the sky. "When Orion slew the Great Bear, its blood dripped on the trees and turned many leaves red. And when he cooked the bear, its fat spattered from the pot and turned the remaining leaves yellow. That's why every autumn the leaves change color."

Tracy deciphered Greg's cryptic explanation even before he reached the moral of his story. "That means you'll tell me this coming autumn."

"You can hold me to it, if things work out the way I hope."

Tracy snuggled deeper against the tree. Even though the temperature had dropped precipitously during the evening, she felt warm and glowing. "A story like that makes you feel closer to the Native Americans, doesn't it?"

"Yes it does. Especially when you realize that until the Spaniards invaded the Southwest looking for the Seven Cities of Cibola, this is all the natives had. They were under the spell of the sky, the land, and their imaginations. The folk tales that resulted were their way of explaining nature."

"Does anyone know where the Seven Cities were located?"

He shook his head. "There are plenty of theories. My own is that they did exist, although not with the fancy trappings the Spaniards expected. There are hundreds of rich gold deposits in the mountains, so it's possible that there were working mines in these mountains many centuries ago. After the mines dried up, the knowledge was handed down for generations. Over many years, the stories grew and became exaggerated. By the time Coronado and his conquistadors arrived, the stories were completely out of proportion to the truth, but the Spaniards were greedy and they fell for them."

"I'd give anything to know what kinds of thoughts were going through the minds of Coronado and his men while they were exploring this land," Tracy said. "Imagine what it must have been like to be separated from their families and friends by a huge ocean and no way of communicating. Did they honestly expect to return home, or were they more realistic and fear they would lose their lives in an alien land?"

"I've thought about that a lot," Greg said. "Most of them were adventurers determined to find a fortune to take back to Spain. Most of the treasure would have to be designated for the courts, but I imagine each man planned to keep something for himself and his family. A few in the group were priests who were authorized by the church to save the natives living here. They firmly believed that they were going among heathens. From the records, we know that Coronado came through what is now Arizona and New Mexico, but little is known about his route. Evidence is bound to turn up one day to prove exactly where he traveled, although maybe not in my lifetime."

"In one of his lectures, Doc mentioned a road called the Coronado Trail. How does that figure in?"

"Probably not at all. There's no evidence that Coronado and his men traveled that particular road. It's just a name given to a state highway near one of the sites Doc worked on several years ago. Originally, it was an animal trail that the natives later followed, so when the state began paving roads back in the 1930s, someone probably decided that tourists might be attracted by a romantic and historic name."

"Where is it?"

"It starts at Springerville on the edge of the White Mountains, about twenty miles east of Juniper Junction, and runs south to Morenci and Clifton. For years, people suggested that Coronado traveled that path because the height would have given him spectacular views of the countryside and allowed him to spot the golden cities at a distance."

"If they really existed," Tracy said.

Greg nodded. "The problem with that route is the difficult climb it would have been for the horses. Even if they managed to scale the heights carrying heavy gear, the elevation might have caused an even more serious problem for the humans."

"Such as ...?"

"Shortness of breath. That would have slowed the procession considerably."

"Your theory makes sense. Well then, if Coronado didn't travel the road people call the Coronado Trail, what route do you think he took?"

"It seems only natural to me that he would have come right across this plateau between the mountains," Greg said. "Aerial photographs show ancient trails leading here from all directions. For centuries, the local tribes traded with other tribes as far east as Texas and as far west as the Pacific Ocean. Traveling across this plateau would have been fairly easy and Coronado would have made better time than along the cliffs. Since this was a major population center during the 16th Century, he could have replenished his supplies here and gotten reliable information about the villages further on."

"What you say seems plausible, but there's no proof, is there?"

"None at all. Still, I'm convinced it'll show up in time," Greg said. "When that happens, the Apaches on this reservation stand to profit because any artifacts the Spaniards left behind will be worth a fortune."

"Like sunken Spanish treasure?"

"Exactly, Tracy, except their treasures have been buried for generations in the soil instead of under the sea." Greg rubbed his hands together. "Right now, I'm beginning to feel as if *I've* been sitting here for centuries. It's so cold, I'm nearly frozen to the bench."

Tracy giggled. "Now that you mention it, my feet are numb."

"That's your common sense telling you it's time to go in."

"Probably, but I love sitting here and watching the sky now that my eyes are adjusted to the dark. It's beautiful!"

Greg smiled. "Now you can appreciate why the natives had a reverence toward nature. I agree that it's beautiful here, but not quite so beautiful as the spot I've picked out for myself."

"Where's that?"

"In the Superstition Mountains outside Phoenix. Matter of fact, I'm having a house built there. It should be ready this fall, and about time, too. I bought the land several years ago and began building the house myself out of native rock. It was too ambitious a project, though. After I admitted to myself that my dreams exceeded reality, I hired a builder to complete it. He's putting in the finishing touches this summer. Even though it turned out to be more complicated than I anticipated, it's worth the wait."

"What's it like?"

"An architect would probably call it contemporary. It's constructed of stone and redwood and it sits on a bluff to catch the view on every side. There's glass all around to give an open feeling and let in the sun and stars, but it's far enough from the nearest neighbor to be completely private."

"It sounds heavenly," Tracy said. "But why such a big house for one person?"

"Oh, it's not for me alone. I wanted a place large enough for a family. I plan to marry soon."

For a moment, Tracy was at a loss for words. "I ... I hadn't realized you were getting married, but I guess I should have figured that out."

His head swiveled toward her. "Why so?" .

"For one thing, you stay aloof from the women at camp."

Tracy caught the smile in his voice as he said, "Not like Bill, who can't keep his hands off them, or off one in particular."

"That wasn't kind, but it's true." As Greg stood and stretched, she added. "Your girl must be crazy about the house."

"I believe she'll like it."

"She hasn't seen it yet?"

Greg shook his head.

"Then she's a very patient woman. I'd be dying to see it. Are you saving it as a wedding present?"

"You might say so."

"Lucky girl!" Stifling a sigh, Tracy was about to rise and head back to the cabin and her warm sleeping bag when Greg clamped a warning hand on her shoulder. Following his gaze, she saw a man and a woman standing about thirty yards distant under the pine boughs, their forms sharply silhouetted against the sky. The scene that appeared at first glance to be a romantic interlude swiftly evolved into one of mutual agitation. Increasingly, the furtive manner in which the couple conferred suggested a motive more sinister than sensual.

Presently, the argument subsided. The woman relinquished her grip on a small package and offered it to the man. He snatched it from her hands, drew from his hip pocket what appeared to be a wallet, and counted out several bills.

As the woman reached out to accept them, Tracy recognized her profile. A gasp welled in her throat as Greg tightened his grip and eased himself back down by her side. Shoulder to shoulder they waited, motionless, to avoid attracting attention. At length, the couple moved off, still engaged in a hushed, but animated, exchange.

"You were right about Woody," Tracy whispered.

Greg nodded. "But I was way off on his accomplice."

"Brenda?"

"That's who it looks like to me."

"It makes no sense for her to be involved in something underhanded."

"Money talks," Greg said. "I would have guessed Diane, or Rosa, even Julia. Brenda is definitely a dark horse."

"Maybe he chose her because she's trustworthy."

"Good point. Still, this shatters that reputation. I gave her credit for having more backbone."

"So did I, but people are surprising. I'm beginning to believe that Juniper Junction is a hotbed of intrigue."

Greg sighed. "The complications are mounting much too quickly. Granted, I feel a responsibility to help the local Apaches to the best of my ability, but there's just so much one person can do to stem the tide of deceit."

"Don't feel that everything falls on your shoulders, Greg. Doc is the one responsible for what happens here, good or bad."

"That's what I keep telling myself. If I were still associated with the university, there might be some basis for staying around, but my job has to come first. The only reason that I've been able to stay in the picture here is my company's generous vacation package. During the year, we travel from one exploration site to another. Because we often have to work seven days a week, they compensate by giving us six weeks off."

"And you spend it here as a trouble shooter instead of doing something selfish, like traveling or resting at the beach. That's very commendable."

"Doc trusted me enough to bring me in on his field school from the outset. Even though he's the authority, I've felt responsible for its reputation."

"But you shouldn't."

"You're absolutely right. I've known all along that the day would come when I'd have to cut the ties and Doc would be left to sink or swim without me. I haven't had the heart to tell him yet, but I think he suspects that this is my last summer at Juniper Junction."

"You have every right to live your own life," Tracy said. "And besides, you're getting married. I don't imagine your wife will want you spending the summer at Juniper Junction. She might have other ideas."

She detected the smile in Greg's voice. "That, too." He rose, towering above her, and held out a hand. "Come along, Tracy. If you sneak back to your cabin now, you'll get there before Brenda. She'll never know you saw her."

Accepting his hand, Tracy marveled at the strength in his grip. "Is this a secret between us, about Brenda and Woody, I mean?"

"Indeed it is. But I'm counting on you to keep your eyes and ears open."

"Believe me, I will."

Greg squeezed her hand. "I know you will. Good night, Tracy."

He strode off in the direction of his cabin while she vainly searched the sky for one more falling star.

Chapter 18

Tracy fell asleep the moment her head touched the pillow. She never heard Brenda return to the cabin, but something aroused her in the middle of a fitful dream. Sitting up with a jerk, she saw Brenda's form outlined on the cot across the room. Just as she was about to settle back, she heard an unmistakable groan. A second moan, accompanied by a sob, was reason enough for Tracy to extricate herself from the sleeping bag. Shivering, she padded across the cold floor.

"Are you sick, Brenda?"

Brenda reached out and clutched Tracy's arm. "Shhhh. Don't wake anyone. Please help me."

"I'll try. What's wrong?" Remembering the surreptitious meeting she and Greg had observed, a dozen possibilities flashed through Tracy's mind. She was not prepared for Brenda's reply.

"I think someone cast a spell on me."

"What are you talking about?"

"An Indian spell. They're powerful."

"You've been having a nightmare. You can't possibly be under a spell."

"But I am. I ache all over, my legs are numb, and my head's throbbing."

"Sounds like a fever to me." Gingerly, Tracy felt Brenda's brow. "Yep, you definitely have a temperature. I'll call Woody."

"No, please don't!" Brenda tried to rise, but fell back helplessly. "I have something medicine can't cure. See, it's black magic."

Before Tracy could react, Brenda pressed several hard objects into her hand. They were impossible to identify in the dark.

"What on earth are these, Brenda?"

"They're sacred artifacts. Someone put a curse on me with them."

"You have a wild imagination. Now I know you're not well."

"No, believe me. It's true! Please don't tell a soul."

"Don't be silly. You've picked up a bug of some kind. I'm going after Woody. Don't worry. Everything will be fine, just fine," Tracy said, not believing one word she uttered.

She drew on her jeans, grabbed her jacket, and ran straightway out the door. At the end of the pine grove, she dashed across the gravel lane without hesitating, scarcely noticing the pain as the rough stones bit the soles of her bare feet.

The cabin that Woody and Shirley shared was dark and foreboding. Tracy rapped on the door. At length, she heard someone stir within. Moments later, the door opened a crack. "What's going on? ... Oh, it's you, Tracy."

"Shirley, I must see Woody right away. It's urgent!"

"Sorry, he's not in."

"Not in? But it's very late. When will he ...?"

"Can't say," Shirley blurted in response to the unfinished question. "He drove over to the Apache village after supper. They're having some sort of pow-wow there."

"But I ...," Tracy stopped short, catching herself from divulging what she had seen. "Brenda has a fever and says her legs are numb."

Shirley's eyes narrowed. "Brenda? Her legs are numb? Is she paralyzed?"

"She didn't make herself clear."

Shirley frowned. "I wonder if she has meningitis. There was a case on the reservation earlier this year. Better get her out of camp before it spreads."

"What should we do?"

"Woody will want to send her to a hospital first thing in the morning. Keep her warm and make sure that the others in your cabin don't get near her."

"Wait a minute! You're a nurse. Surely you can handle the situation better than I can."

"You'll do just fine." Shirley said. "Besides, you've already been exposed to whatever she has. If I became contaminated, then I could pass it along to the others. When Woody gets back, I'll let him know what's happened. He'll contact a local hospital."

Bewildered and angered by Shirley's refusal to accept responsibility in what loomed as an emergency, and certain that Woody was in the cabin, listening to every word, Tracy turned and fled across the grass, oblivious of her course until she found herself before the cabin of the one person in camp who would help.

Furtively, she tapped on the cabin window. On an earlier evening, she had seen his figure outlined by the glow of lanterns inside the cabin and concluded that his bed was against the adjacent wall. Now she prayed that she was not mistakenly rousing the wrong person.

Seconds later, she heard the door squeak open and his voice speak her name, as if he were expecting her. "Tracy? What on earth …?"

"Greg, please come! Something awful happened!"

He did not ask what had happened or why Tracy was summoning him. He simply said, "Hold on. I'll be right there."

In less than a minute, he was by her side, still buttoning his shirt. "Where to?"

"My cabin. It's Brenda."

Tracy felt Greg take her arm, completely in command. He walked briskly, pulling her along with him until they reached the gravel road. She hesitated.

He glanced down at her feet. "Good heavens, Tracy! Why aren't you wearing your boots?"

Not waiting for her answer, he scooped her up and carried her across the road. Gently setting her back on the ground, he said, "Now give, Tracy. What's wrong."

"Brenda might have meningitis."

He grabbed her arm. "Where did you get that idea?"

"She has a fever and she says her legs are numb. Shirley Morgan says …"

"Shirley? You spoke with Shirley? What about Woody?"

"Shirley says he's not there, and she won't become involved. She says I've already been exposed and it's best that I stay with Brenda until she can get to a hospital."

Greg whistled. "So much for honesty among thieves. All right, Tracy. It's you and me. We'll bumble through somehow. First we'll move her from the cabin to the infirmary. How strong are you?"

"Like a rock, after digging all summer."

"Atta girl. We'll use the stretcher in the infirmary. Can you manage one end?"

"I'll have to, won't I?"

He shot her an encouraging smile. "You'll do fine. Wait here. I'll be right back."

Tracy followed the sound of his fading footsteps as he ran toward the infirmary. Several minutes passed before he returned, bursting through the pines, the stretcher in his grip. He motioned her to follow him to the cabin.

At the doorway, she tugged on his sleeve. "Be very quiet. Brenda doesn't want the others to know. She thinks it's an Indian spell."

He started to say something, then thought better of it.

They entered and tiptoed to Brenda's cot.

Tracy spoke in a whisper. "We're back."

"Who's with you?" Brenda's voice quivered.

"Greg."

"Greg? But he can't ..."

"Shhh! Greg knows exactly what to do. We're moving you to the infirmary. Can you roll over onto this stretcher?"

Brenda surrendered without protest. "I ... I think so."

Greg bent down and whispered in Tracy's ear. "First get something on your feet." Obediently, she located the boots from underneath her cot and sat down long enough to tug them on. Once shod, she returned to the task at hand. With a minimum of assistance from the patient, Tracy and Greg shifted Brenda onto the stretcher and quit the cabin as silently as cat burglars. At the infirmary, they transferred Brenda to a low bed.

Greg straightened up. "I'll call from the office phone. You'll be okay while I'm gone, Tracy?"

She nodded. He patted her shoulder, then left.

Tracy was bathing Brenda's face in cool water when Greg returned and dropped into a chair. "I managed to reach the university hospital. They'll dispatch a plane to pick her up."

"A plane? You really can work wonders. When will it be here?"

"By two o'clock, three at the outset. It could take several hours to get a team together, but the flight's under a half hour. I set out a lantern on the field behind the dining hall. How's she doing?"

"Fine," Tracy said. She saw no improvement, but did not want to say anything to alarm Brenda.

Brenda groaned. "Where are they?"

"They're coming soon," Greg said.

"The fetishes, I mean. What did you do with them?"

Tracy fumbled in her jacket pocket for the objects. Locating them, she drew them out for Brenda to see.

Brenda recoiled. "Get rid of them!"

Greg reached out and plucked them from Tracy's hand. He examined them under the light. "Typical fetishes. Walnut shell rattles and a carved cat, probably a puma."

Tracy frowned. "Do you believe there really is sorcery involved?"

He shrugged. "Depends on how you look at it."

"How do *you* look at it?"

"Professionally, I regard them as cultural relics, but I have great respect for any artifact that the natives value as a religious icon."

"Isn't that a conflict of beliefs?"

"I don't think so. You and I believe in a higher being. Most often, we pray for help in becoming better humans, and when we're feeling greedy, we might ask for certain material items, or for certain events to take place. The difference between our religion and those practiced by natives of America, Africa, and the islands is that they worship several elements of nature. The early European settlers called them heathens and to this day they're often accused of practicing magic or worshiping the supernatural. We forget that they might look at us the same way."

"How so?"

"The forms of nature they worship are visible or tangible, whereas we revere an unseen being. From their point of view, our deity has even more supernatural qualities than theirs. I know of prayers that our invisible god has answered, even some of my own." He gave an embarrassed chuckle. "For that matter, I've seen supernatural charms work just as well, sometimes to do harm rather than good."

"Surely you don't think that Brenda has anything to fear?"

Greg smiled wryly. "The Native Americans have the uncanny ability to correlate the everyday with the mystical. They're especially skilled at scaring off demons, but they can turn them loose on others just as easily."

Tracy eyed the fetishes in Greg's palm. "What do you think these are used for?"

"It's hard to tell. Let's see if Brenda is any help." He leaned over the bed. "Where did you get these, Brenda?"

Brenda peered up at him, fear in her eyes. "I can't tell you."

Greg and Tracy exchanged glances. "Then I'll have to assume it was Woody," he said. "Am I right?"

"No. That's not true."

"He was in on it, though, wasn't he?"

"What do you mean?" Brenda suddenly seemed to be more terrified of Greg's question than of her health.

"I'm talking about whatever you two are involved in. Something's going on. We know that much."

Brenda burst into tears. "It wasn't my idea."

"What wasn't your idea?"

"The stones ..." Brenda began, then gasped in dismay, realizing that she had given herself away.

Greg smacked his lips. "Aha! So you're in on the fire agate smuggling?"

Brenda's response came in a weak whisper. "Y ... y ... yes."

"Then tell me how Woody is involved."

"I don't know."

"Surely you don't expect me to believe that."

"Honestly," Brenda said. "I don't know. I just give them to him and he pays me."

A quizzical expression spread across Greg's face. "He pays *you*? Let's start from the beginning. If Woody pays you, where do you get the agates?"

"From Alice Quail Run. She lives in the Apache village."

Tracy grabbed Greg's sleeve. "She must be the one who left the package at the lab."

Brenda tried to raise her head off the pillow. "Someone left a package? Do you have it?"

Tracy nodded.

Brenda sank back on the pillow, relieved. "You've got to give it to Woody right away. He's furious with me. And so is Alice."

Greg tossed a meaningful glance at Tracy before turning back to Brenda. "Where does Alice get the agates?"

"She steals them, I guess."

Tracy's mouth flew open. "Steals them! Why would she do that?"

"I give her a portion of my share. She needs the money for her children. She knows the secret place where the tribe stores the agates they mine, so she takes them to sell because her little boy's a cripple, and the baby is always sick. Alice coughs a lot herself."

"Probably tuberculosis," Greg said. "Native Americans are susceptible to it because of constant exposure to the elements and poor sanitation. The squalid living conditions most of them endure would kill the rest of us in short order."

Tracy folded her arms and confronted Brenda. "Now we know why Alice is willing to steal, but how and why did *you* get involved?"

"Woody needed someone as a go-between."

"We get the picture," Greg said. "I suppose Shirley recruited you out on the dig, but now she refuses to help. It's probably more about fear of being linked with the thefts than fear of contamination. Now what do you know about the way Woody disposes of the gems?"

"It's a big operation. Lots of people. Like a chain."

Tracy leaned over to wipe the perspiration from Brenda's face, as Greg continued to grill her. "Can I assume that others at Juniper Junction are involved?"

Brenda hesitated. "Maybe so, but Woody and Shirley told me that every link has to act alone and can't be responsible for the fate of the others."

"That's a great attitude," Greg said, unable to veil his disgust. "All right, Brenda, you might not know who else is involved beside the Morgans, but you certainly can explain why you and Woody were arguing earlier this evening."

Brenda's eyes widened. "You saw us? It was about that delivery. I slipped once and told Alice that the money came from a doctor, so when I wasn't on time for my pick-up at the mile marker, she came all the way here to deliver them. She said that she left her village when nobody was around, but she was afraid to go back home with them for fear of being caught. Terrible things would happen if a shaman or elder sensed that she had them."

"Such as becoming the object of a curse," Greg said.

Brenda's expression radioed defeat. "Yes, exactly. Except I'm the one who got it instead."

"I don't understand how that could happen," Tracy said.

"When Woody didn't get his delivery, he sent me to Alice for it. Neither of us knew at the time that she already had delivered it. She thought that he was trying to cheat her, so she decided to end the arrangement."

"But the medicine man," Tracy said. "How did he become involved?"

"There was no medicine man," Brenda said. "Alice performed the magic herself."

"Most natives know a storehouse of magic," Greg explained to Tracy. "Even though many join our churches and accept our religion, they retain the old ways."

"I see," Tracy said. "I suppose they regard magic as a reliable back-up. In this case, what did Alice do?"

"She must have gotten hold of something belonging to me, maybe something as small as a loose hair," Brenda said. "Then she probably went through the usual incantations calling on the spirits to send me bad luck. When she completed the spell, she must have crept into our cabin while we were out on the dig and put those in my bed." Brenda gestured weakly toward the objects.

Tracy was skeptical. "Alice seemed like a very nice lady. I have trouble believing that she would weave a spell capable of harming another human being so decisively. That's pretty far-fetched. Even if she had gone through the exercise, how would she know which cabin and which bed were yours? And what benefit would it be to her for you to become paralyzed?"

"I don't know, but it happened." Brenda squeezed her eyelids shut to stem the flow of tears.

Tracy turned to Greg. "Do you believe what she's saying?"

"Who am I to question native magic? It's strong stuff."

"Then if this rattle and piece of rock made Brenda sick, how do we know that we won't be harmed the same way by handling them?"

"We don't, but the chances are slim. Alice probably has nothing belonging to you, Tracy. Even if she does, you've done nothing to enrage her, have you?"

Tracy detected a sly smile. "I think you're spoofing, Greg."

The smile widened. "I'm a practical man, Tracy, but some psychologists recognize a strong relationship between spells cast and harm befalling the intended victims. They give it a fancy term: Synchronicity."

Tracy shrugged. "Whatever that means."

"It means that it's not a coincidence Brenda became ill after she began believing that Alice cast a spell on her. The victim of a spell subconsciously expects the magic to work and it does, or seems to. Common sense flies out the window. Basically, folks who believe they're under a spell behave accordingly. Their physical reactions seem real. They're like hypochondriacs who take on the symptoms of diseases they think they have, but don't."

Spell or no, Tracy observed that Brenda seemed visibly ill. She changed the cold compresses several times and offered frequent sips of water that Brenda accepted greedily. In time, Brenda slept. While Tracy adjusted the bed covers, Greg fired up logs in the stone fireplace. Only when the flames erupted did Tracy realize how cold and tired she was. Pulling a blanket from the cabinet, she wrapped it around herself and stumbled into a chair directly before the hearth.

Chapter 19

The next thing Tracy knew, someone was shaking her shoulder gently. She opened her eyes and saw Greg standing before her. Steam spiraled from the mug he held and a delicious aroma filled the air.

"I didn't mean to waken you," he said. "I thought you were just resting your eyes. Would you like some coffee?"

Tracy accepted the mug eagerly and took a sip of its delectable contents. "You're a mind reader," she said. "This is delicious! You beat Clarence any day. How did you learn to brew coffee like this?"

"Pure necessity," Greg said. "I like good coffee, and since I have to fend for myself, I learned to do it properly. When you grow up in an orphanage, you become self-sufficient very early."

Tracy nearly dropped the cup. "Orphanage! You're an orphan? I've never known an orphan."

"Well, you know one now," he said lightly, overlooking the remark that Tracy knew was trite and thoughtless, even as the words tumbled from her lips.

"If you're an orphan, how did you manage to become a geologist?"

He grinned broadly. "Orphans are people, too."

"But you don't have a family for support," Tracy said, unable to stem the inane comments streaming from her mouth.

"On the contrary, I have a huge family. Lots of brothers, none of them related to me of course, but all good friends." He laughed aloud. "Don't look so shocked, Tracy."

"I'm not shocked, just amazed by what you've accomplished and furious with myself for reacting so childishly. It's an honor to know someone who'd be a star candidate for an article or book, even a movie, about a waif who makes good." She buried her head in her hands. "The more I say, the more ignorant I sound!"

His smile was kindly. "Your reaction is perfectly normal. Don't demean yourself unnecessarily."

She turned scarlet, aware that Greg was studying her intently. For the first time, she read the searching look in his eyes as loneliness and, for one brief second, she was tempted to reach out and clasp a small, homeless boy in her arms. But when she looked again, she saw the capable, assured man that he was and she remembered that he would soon marry and begin his own family. Tracy hoped he could not penetrate her thoughts.

Casually, she said, "What else do you cook? If you do as well with everything else, your wife won't have to spend much time in the kitchen."

"I wouldn't mind. She'll probably want a career of her own. If so, I'll be glad to help with the meals. I like to cook."

"So do I, but it's not much fun by myself. After my mother died, I cooked for my father, but ever since he remarried …" Tracy's voice trailed off. She took another sip of the rich coffee, warming her hands and trying to clear her mind at the same time.

Greg dropped down at her feet to face the fire, drawing his knees up to his chin. Silently, they basked in the luxury of the flames that cast long, eerie shadows toward the dark corner where Brenda lay. At length, Tracy drained her mug and sat it carefully on the floor. For all its stark furnishings, the infirmary seemed oddly cheerful. Greg rose and tossed another log on the fire. As the sparks hissed and vaulted up the chimney, their red glow seemed to heighten his cheekbones. Tracy saw his jaw tighten, his temple pulse throb, and she knew that his thoughts paralleled hers.

"What will we tell the others about …?"

"Nothing." His voice was firm, authoritative.

"Nothing?"

"Nothing beyond Brenda's emergency. That's legitimate. Regardless of whether her illness is caused by natural forces or native mumbo-jumbo, there'll be plenty of talk, enough to distract Woody and anyone else who's worried that we're onto something."

"What if the fire agate smuggling continues?"

"I predict they'll stay low for a while. Remember, their go-between is now out of the picture. I doubt that Woody will make personal contact with Alice so long as he thinks Brenda's capable of talking. In the meantime, I'll try to get a better picture of Alice's situation through one of my Apache friends and see if there is something to be done for her family so she doesn't have to resort to crime."

"But what about Doc? Will you tell him?"

Greg grew thoughtful. "As soon as I decide on the right approach."

"You're fond of Doc, aren't you, even though he's not quite so perfect as the rest of the world believes?"

"He's been good to me," Greg said.

"How long have you known him?"

"Since my early teens. He came around to the orphanage on weekends to help out in the sports program and took an interest in me. I was a fairly accurate quarterback, and I was tall besides, so he saw the potential and began working with me regularly. As a result, I led my school team to an undefeated season, and I got a football scholarship to the university, probably thanks to a few strings Doc pulled. I made the varsity squad my sophomore year, and by the time I was a senior, I'd done well enough to interest the pros, but by then I'd discovered geology. That promised a steadier future. The bloated salary I'd pull in for a few years with the pros couldn't compensate for acquiring knowledge that would benefit me for a lifetime, so I entered graduate school and survived financially by working part-time for Doc. The athletic training wasn't lost, though, because now I spend my free time working with youth groups."

Tracy studied Greg's face. He was at once serious and honest, completely devoid of guile, and about as devoted as a puppy dog. She could not resist returning his smile. "Tell me everything you do back in the real world, when you're not running interference for Doc."

He seemed pleased. "You don't have to coax, Tracy. Even if you're not all that interested, it may help get your mind off Brenda. First, how about some more coffee?"

"Marvelous." Tracy studied his face as he filled her cup. Why, she wondered, was she shivering even though the coffee and the fire had warmed her hands and feet?

Over cups of steaming coffee laced with thick cream from the reservation cattle, they talked in low voices. Greg explained his duties with the oil company, how he sought potential sites for exploration and supervised the drilling. And when Tracy's expression signaled that he was talking over her head, he patiently restated everything in simplified terms.

"I like to believe I'm doing a service when I locate a shale or coal deposit," he said. "The only problem with the job is the time it involves. There's lots of travel and no end of eighteen-hour days, but that's been good for me. I put in so much overtime that I usually earn enough extra leave every year to help Doc for a week or so beyond the six weeks of camp that my vacation covers."

"That's being devoted beyond the call of duty," Tracy said. "By giving him your free time, he's the only one benefiting from your sacrifice. Here at camp you do most of the lab work, you fight the forest fires, you cover up for Doc when he cheats in his findings, and tonight you're taking on the responsibility the camp doctor should cover. Do you think it's fair of Doc to let you do all his worrying just so he can hang onto his reputation?"

Greg grinned. "You certainly have a way of getting right to the point, Tracy. When you put it that way, it makes me see things in a new light. The answer is a definite no. Doc has his life to live, and I have mine. It's to everyone's advantage that I bow out after this season. When I have time away from work in the future, I want to spend it with my wife. And now this on top of everything." He motioned toward Brenda. "Gem smuggling is much too dicey for me."

"Even though you're on the trail of the culprits?"

"Especially because I am. The trail may lead too far."

"Too near, you mean," Tracy said. Their eyes met.

For more than an hour, they talked about everything that came to mind: their dissimilar childhoods, their likes and dislikes, their fears, even their hopes and dreams, and they found themselves laughing together in spite of the circumstances. Not until the sound of an approaching airplane cut through their conversation did Tracy take stock of where they were, and why.

Greg jumped up and ran out to guide the pilot to a landing spot. As the roar of the engine broke the deathly stillness of camp, Tracy quivered with fear. It would not do for the others to waken and learn the terrible secret. But that never happened. The pilot waited at the controls while Greg and the medic shifted Brenda onto a stretcher and carried her from the infirmary to the plane. Once she was on board, the door closed. Moments later, the plane taxied across the mesa.

Tracy and Greg watched it lift off and slowly gather altitude. When its lights were no longer visible, hidden from sight by the towering mountains, they returned to the infirmary to bank the fire.

"There are bound to be questions tomorrow," Tracy said. "What shall I say?"

"Nothing but the truth. We'll tell anyone who asks that Brenda became ill, but leave it at that without elaborating. It could be downright dangerous."

"What if your cabin mates hear you come in?"

Greg grinned down at her. "I'll be truthful and tell them I had a late date."

Tracy blushed.

Greg's eyes danced. "Surely you don't mind if I regard these pleasant hours together as an assignation?"

She grinned back. "Not if you think your girl doesn't mind."

"From everything I know about her, I guarantee she trusts me."

Tracy laughed. "I'll vouch for that, even in elevators. And Greg …?"

"Yes?"

She held out her hand. "Thank you, for everything."

Solemnly, he accepted her hand and gave it a parting squeeze. "The thanks are all mine, Tracy. Now hurry on back and get some rest. The sun will rise before you know it."

"You, too."

"Remember, play it cool at breakfast. See you then."

In the morning, Tracy behaved with exaggerated nonchalance, casually informing her cabin mates and several others that Brenda had become sick during the night and arrangements had been made for her removal to the university hospital. Greg's name never surfaced; nearly everyone seemed to assume that Woody had taken command of the situation. They could not have guessed otherwise, unless they happened to observe the bitter glances Greg shot across the breakfast table to Woody and Shirley, or saw the doctor's hand tremble when he served himself a pancake, his eyes averted from Greg's, as if mesmerized by a syrup puddle on his plate.

Even Julia, usually suspicious and apprehensive, mumbled a few words of regret about Brenda's illness, then downed her meal with ample gusto for one watching her figure. Her reaction convinced Tracy that she was not the least troubled by the incident. Ironically, and blessedly, so far as Tracy was concerned, Brenda's fate took second billing to the major news of the morning: Bill's hasty departure. To Tracy's relief, he left camp shortly after breakfast, saying that he needed to be with Tish to help complete their wedding plans.

Before heading for the truck, Tracy returned to the cabin to collect her hat, canteen, and log book, then stopped by the lab for the notebook that she had turned in for evaluation after Doc's most recent lecture. It lay in the bin, still unmarked. This did not surprise her, since neither Doc nor Greg had much opportunity during the week to do any grading. Leaving the notebook where it was, she started toward the door when her attention was captured by low, urgent voices coming from Doc's office. She paused, straining to hear, and immediately recognized Greg's voice. He was saying something about Woody. Although Tracy could not make out every word, she knew he was presenting vivid reasons why Doc should sever his relationship with a criminal.

She drew closer to the office door. "It's just a matter of time before he's found out," she heard Greg say. "When that scandal breaks, it won't look good for any professional who works closely with him. Permitting him to finish out the summer in camp is about as close to trouble as you can get. You'll be guilty by association."

"You realize of course, Greg, that I have to provide proper medical care for the camp, so it may be difficult to find a qualified person willing to come for the rest of the term."

"That's a feeble excuse, Doc. You know plenty of physicians who would jump at the chance for a free vacation in the woods. All you have to do is contact the university hospital and you'll have a dozen applicants here within a day."

"So you're asking me to put friendship aside and tell an old pal that he and his wife have to leave?"

"I'm not asking, I'm telling you." Greg's voice was stern. "It's for your own good. The longer he stays, the more difficult it will be for you to avoid the spotlight."

Doc heaved a deep sigh. "You're right. You're always right. I'll speak to him just as soon as I can do it tactfully."

"Tactfully!" Tracy sensed that Greg was about to explode, but he managed to check himself and maintain a low, controlled voice. She caught occasional words, among them Brenda's name, and her own. Each time Greg stopped for breath, Doc replied in a monosyllable. Becoming more fascinated by the minute, Tracy crept forward until she was close enough to hear Greg say, "I feel completely responsible for her. After all, I brought her here, and I won't let anyone put her on the spot. Not even you!"

Amusement colored Doc's voice as he said, "It sounds to me as if you feel something more for her than mere responsibility."

"Get back to the point! We're talking about you, Doc, your behavior. You're not a kid. If you don't care about wrecking your personal life, then think about this camp and the people here!"

There was a long pause before Doc responded. "It looks like you have the upper hand now, Greg, but then I never tried to make you believe I'm perfect, did I? Well, we'll hope that everything turns out well for Brenda. As for Tracy …"

"As for her, I want your solemn promise …"

With that, Greg's voice became inaudible. The next thing Tracy heard was Doc saying, "It's as good as done."

Hearing no response from Greg, Tracy concluded that the exchange was over. She edged back toward the door so they would not discover her eavesdropping, but in her haste she brushed against a stool. The sound of it sliding along the bare wooden floor gave away her presence. As the office door swung wide, Tracy instinctively turned herself around so it appeared that she had just entered the building.

"Why, Tracy, good morning." Doc's voice was deep and smooth without a trace of the drama she had overheard. "Can I help you?"

"Thanks, Doc. I was coming to see if my notebook's been marked." She made a pretense of walking to the bin and leafing through the pages. "No, I see it's not ready. That's all right. I'll pick it up later."

"I'm sorry I haven't had a chance to get to them," Doc said. He turned to Greg. "How about you? Think you'll have time to check Tracy's notebook today?"

Greg cast a knowing glance at Tracy over Doc's shoulder. "If I don't have any more interruptions," he said.

"That will be fine," Tracy said. "See you both later. I'd better get to the truck before it leaves." With that, she dashed past Doc and out the door.

Chapter 20

Later that afternoon, Tracy was squatting on the ground extracting bits of pottery from the shovel loads of soil Becky tossed against the screen when the distant hum of a motor caught her attention. She rose to stretch just as Greg's truck crested the rise.

"Greg's coming a bit early," she said.

"Maybe he's bringing us leftovers from lunch," Becky said. "I could do with a snack."

"I'm afraid you'll be disappointed." Tracy said, as she watched the truck veer sharply away from them. "It looks as if he has something else in mind."

"Darn it!" Becky stood, shielding her eyes from the sun. "I thought you were fooling me, but you're right. He's going toward the cowboys."

"Cowboys?"

"Or whatever you call the Apaches on horseback." Becky pointed toward tiny figures at the far side of the plain.

"Oh, I can see them now. They were so far away it was hard to make them out."

"Why do you suppose he's going after them?"

"Probably he just wants to be friendly," Tracy said, careful to speak casually in the improbable case that Becky was involved in the fire agate scheme. "I imagine that they were some of the crew who helped out at the fire. You know men. They like to talk about past conquests."

She was certain, however, that his primary motive was to learn if tribal members knew about Alice's visit to camp and, if so, to devise a way of alleviating their suspicions.

Accepting Tracy's explanation, Becky returned to her task, but Tracy continued to monitor Greg's truck until she saw it stop a short distance from the riders. They hailed him in friendship and waited while he jumped out and strode toward them. Once it was evident that the men were deep in earnest conversation, she dropped to the ground and resumed sorting the artifacts trapped by the screen.

By the time Tracy finished bagging and recording her findings, Greg had pulled up, ready to load their materials into the truck. He said little, but Tracy read his quiet smile as a sign of reassurance that he was working on the problem at hand. She and Becky clambered into the front seat, and once he covered the load in the bed with a tarp, he slid in beside her.

Becky minced no words. "We saw you driving toward the cowboys. Do you know them?"

If Greg was surprised, the tone of his voice was pure calm. "Yes, I've known them for several years, since I've been coming to camp. They're very nice fellows, brothers who work hard to eke out an existence. Both have families who could use our help."

"What kind of help?" Tracy asked.

She felt the nudge of Greg's elbow as he said, "Health care, for a start. One of them has a little boy who has trouble walking, a baby who cries constantly, and a wife who may be in the early stages of tuberculosis. The other one recently lost a child to a high fever. I told them to bring their families to Woody."

Tracy easily identified Alice and her children as belonging to the first Apache. She wondered if Greg would divulge their secret in front of Becky, but he calmed her fear with a second nudge and a wink. Recovering, she said, "That's a very good idea."

"Especially since nobody in camp is sick and he seems to have a lot of time on his hands," Greg said.

Becky laughed. "Boy, will he be annoyed. I get the impression that he'd do anything to avoid work. He's not a stellar representative of his profession."

Greg's elbow dug into Tracy's ribs once more. "It appears that the good doctor hasn't pulled the wool over everyone's eyes."

Tracy smiled up at him. She was beginning to think that he was capable of solving all the world's woes, or those visited upon Juniper Junction at the very least.

The very next evening, Doc announced at supper that Woody had volunteered to help several families in the Apache village who were in need of medical services. Tracy acknowledged a sly glance from Greg across the room, then turned away quickly. It would not do for others to suspect that they were in collusion. She wondered if Greg had approached Woody directly, or if Doc was the wielder of strong-arm tactics. Whatever the method of forced encouragement, Woody and Shirley accepted compliments from those seated nearby who seemed visibly impressed by their commitment to the less fortunate. The brazen smirk on Woody's face broadcast his triumph at slithering out of trouble this time as easily as he must have done in the past. She wondered what conditions Doc had presented. Nothing in his voice hinted a rift between the two or condemnation of the physician's behavior.

"It's a pleasure to know that our colleagues are dedicated to serving the needy," Doc said. "The folks on this reservation don't see many doctors, so the adults develop chronic illnesses and the children grow up with problems that could have been treated and cured. I'm pleased to report that Woody visited the village this afternoon to assess their needs. As a result, he's ordered some medicines from the pharmacy in Globe. We're in luck because Snakeskin is leaving tomorrow to pick up supplies there. He'll bring back the medicines and a leg brace, along with all the things we need."

Julia seated next to him seemed startled. "A leg brace?"

Doc looked down at her. "For a little boy in the village. Woody tells me that it will help him get around and in time will strengthen his leg enough so that he can walk on his own."

"That's the nicest thing Woody has done since I've known him," Julia said, flashing a smile that Tracy knew at once was as false as her eyelashes. "From the way he treats this camp like a vacation spot, I was beginning to think he was oblivious to the less fortunate, but this unexpected kindness gives me a much different picture. Perhaps he really does believe in the Hippocratic oath." The last remark was coated with sarcasm.

An uncomfortable silence passed over the dining room before Doc rescued the situation. "Julia has a delightful sense of humor. It goes without saying that both of us are deeply indebted to Woody and Shirley for giving up their free time to keep everyone in camp healthy. If it weren't for them, this place could look like an emergency ward. We've been fortunate that nobody here has had anything more than a few scrapes and sprains these past few summers."

While Doc was speaking, Tracy caught Julia's eye. As the summer progressed it was becoming apparent to her that the older woman had a sharp mind. Instead of settling into the guise of a brainless ornament that Doc enjoyed displaying to enhance his prestige, Julia knew exactly what was going on around her. Rather than reveal her distaste for some of Doc's projects and the people who kowtowed to him, she had been clever enough thus far to submerge her true feelings, but her remark that caught Doc momentarily without a comeback opened a crack in her cool façade. Tracy shot Julia a smile of approval, hoping it was subtle enough for others to ignore even as it commended Julia's decision to speak out.

Julia looked directly at Tracy. Her lips curved into a faint smile, a signal that she regarded the younger woman as an ally. No words passed between them, yet her meaning was clear.

At the same time, Woody drew attention to himself by waving his hand in the air until the kitchen crew quieted down and private conversations ceased. "Hey there, folks, I thank Doc for those kind words and support," he said. "Shirley and I've been coming here long enough for you to know that we love Juniper Junction and look forward to each summer. You're the greatest bunch of folks ever. You've given us some of the best days of our lives. Now we have the opportunity to do a bit of charity work for the local community and we're really grateful for the privilege."

Tracy could not help glancing over at Greg. She knew by the pained expression on his face that he was struggling to avoid blurting the remark lodged on the tip of his tongue. It was within his power to destroy Doc, as well as Woody.

Before the evening lecture began, he paused by her chair. Without looking directly at her, he spoke in a voice too low to be noticed by others. "The wheels turn quickly once they're greased, but they don't turn far enough. Some people don't have the courage to throw out the trash."

Tracy tore off a sheet of notebook paper and wrote: Charity trumps expulsion?

Greg glanced over her shoulder at the sheet, nodded, and moved away to set up the projector.

The next few days were blissfully calm for Tracy. There was so little left to complete on the strat test that she volunteered to finish it alone. That freed Becky to return to the broadside, where Doc wanted to pull out all stops before summer's end. Even better, it enabled Tracy to avoid involvement with members of the gem ring, whoever they were. Engrossed in thoughts about Brenda, Doc and others, she dug and sifted mechanically until mid-afternoon of the third day when a shadow fell across her excavation. Looking up, she saw Greg, his hat shoved back to reveal a shock of damp, dark hair. Tracy had been so lost in thought she had not heard his truck drive alongside the pit.

His eyes were apologetic. "I didn't mean to frighten you, but I wanted you to know …"

"It's about Brenda," Tracy said, before he could finish.

"Yep. She's been released from the hospital. The report says she had some kind of viral infection. That confirms my suspicions."

"Wait a minute! You had me believing that her explanation about the curse was legitimate."

He smiled. "Don't believe everything you hear, Tracy. A scientist insists on tangible proof. With the amulets out of the picture, the crux of her problem can be summed up as a classic case of hypochondria."

"So what happens to her?"

"According to my source, she's in good health, but she's not coming back to camp."

"I shouldn't wonder. I suspect that she wants to run as far as she can to avoid arrest."

"That's assuming the story breaks," Greg said. "Plans are underway to make amends quickly. If that happens, maybe nothing more will come of it."

Tracy shook her head in dismay. "What a mess! Never in my wildest dreams could I have conjured up a summer like this one."

"It must be a big disappointment for you."

"That's an understatement. It's some consolation that Woody is being forced to atone for his crimes by doing good deeds for the families in the village. I saw Snakeskin unloading the kitchen supplies from his truck the other evening when he got back from Globe. I didn't have a chance to ask him, but I assume he brought back the medicine."

"Enough to last the village a long time. We'll leave it with the elders when we pull up stakes. They'll dole it out as needed."

"What about the leg brace? Did Snakeskin get it?"

"Not only did he get it, but Doc drove over to the village a little while ago to pick up Alice and her children and bring them to the infirmary. The last I saw, Woody was fitting the brace on Charlie, Alice's little boy."

"So good things are happening after all," Tracy said. "I'd feel even better if we could somehow get the fire agates Alice delivered back where they belong before anyone suspects that she took them."

Greg grinned. "Ask and ye shall receive."

"Exactly what does that mean?"

"Fret no more. Problem solved. I drove down to the village yesterday and returned them to her. Her husband and the other men were all out on the range, so nobody saw me. A couple of women and children were peering out of the wickiups, but they're notoriously secretive. I'm sure they aren't aware of what happened. Even if they are, they would never tattle on another woman in the village. Alice promised me that she'd return the agates to the storage place at her first opportunity."

Tracy beamed up at him. "How very kind of you to do that. Julia was right."

Greg frowned. "Julia?"

Tracy laughed. She had no intention of divulging her interpretation of the conversation that initially puzzled her the night of the square dance. Now she knew exactly what Julia meant. "She mentioned that you have a reputation for taking matters into your own hands. I know that she meant it in a very nice way."

"That's a surprise. She's not very forthcoming. Still, she might not have meant it the way you think. That brings me to the other reason I'm here."

"And what might that be?"

Hesitating, Greg removed his hat and twirled it around in his hands. "I really hate to ask you, Tracy, but there are specific matters that need attention if the university is to get a record of all the work done in Juniper Junction this summer. I was wondering …"

"Yes?"

"Look, please feel free to refuse if you want to, but I thought I'd ask, just in case …"

"Well for goodness said, stop stalling and ask me, Greg."

Greg inhaled deeply. "The thing is, we're getting down to the wire and the work in the lab is doubling with so much material coming in from the sites. Since nobody else knows what they're dong in there …"

Tracy did not let him finish. "You want me to help you? I'll be glad to."

Greg gulped. "You mean it?"

"Yes, I mean it. I'm sick to death of being out here by myself. And what's even worse, as soon as I finish here, Doc thinks it would be a great idea to move me back near the pueblo. He told me he has a *hunch* I'll find more turquoise there."

Greg caught that easily. "Whew! Can't let that happen, can we?"

"Now do you see why your offer sounds to me like a heavenly reprieve?"

Greg's smile deepened. "Since that's settled, let's see what we can do about getting you out of here ahead of schedule." So saying, he proffered a hand and hoisted Tracy out of the hole.

Her protest was lame. "But I'm not down to native soil yet."

"You will be when I finish," he said.

With that, Greg jumped into the pit and began shoveling mounds of dirt against the screen. As fast as they came, Tracy poked through the debris too coarse to pass through the sieve. Except for some colorful rocks and a few stray animal bones, she saw nothing to interest Doc or any other archaeologist. By late afternoon, true to his word, Greg had cleaned out every speck of earth in the hole right down to the hard native core. For her part, Tracy had bagged and labeled everything worth taking back to the lab. As Greg sat on the edge of the excavation guzzling the dregs of his canteen, Tracy began to giggle. Both of them were filthy and the sight of Greg's white teeth gleaming against his blacked face sent Tracy into gales of laughter.

"I'm glad your spirits are rising," Greg said, wiping his forehead with his bandanna. "The way the summer's been going, I was beginning to think you were a prime candidate for the funny farm."

"You look so awful, I can't help it," Tracy said.

"My appearance may amuse you, but have you any idea how scruffy *you* look?"

Tracy assessed herself hastily, from her clumpy, mud-caked boots to her bedraggled hayseed hat. When her eyes again met Greg's, the two could not help themselves. Laughing like merry rubes, they set about dismantling the site and loading Tracy's equipment into the truck. Just as they were about to leave, Tracy remembered the log book she had secured under a rock. As if on signal, both began racing to the spot.

Greg arrived first and was about to snatch it up when he looked back and saw that Tracy was running toward him on a collision course. Instinctively, he opened his arms and caught her, holding her vice-like, as he had done once before. This time, Tracy was not on the defensive. At the precise moment her heart lurched, she gasped aloud.

Greg was startled. "I'm sorry, Tracy. Did I hurt you?"

"No. I just ... lost my balance," she said, lifting her face to his.

Abruptly, Greg released her, swept up the log from the ground, and presented it to her in awkward silence. By the time they reached the truck, their conversation was flowing naturally. From Tracy's perspective, Greg seemed his usual self, but she was shaking uncontrollably. She prayed he did not notice.

Chapter 21

When Greg announced that Tracy had agreed to help in the lab, Doc merely shrugged and said he would save the new site for the following summer. The next morning, Tracy traded her pick and shovel for a magnifying glass, pottery cement, and a niche in the lab to help Greg amass the information gathered from the various sites at Juniper Junction.

From the outset, she found the lab work so fulfilling that it was hard to recall why she once objected. Everything clicked into focus, as if a giant hand from above was directing the summer's dig. One by one, the teams concluded their field work and moved into the lab to sort out their findings under her supervision. Greg, hunched over his desk, handled his own priorities.

As the materials from Forestdale accumulated, he applied dendrochronology to date the wooden posts from the pit houses. The process looked terribly complicated to Tracy, but when she paused to marvel at the conclusions he reached, he smiled and motioned her to sit down next to him. Step by step, he took her through the tests. Once he let her try her hand.

"Good girl!" He rewarded her success with a pat on the back. "I'd hire you on my team any day."

Tracy excused herself hurriedly, afraid he could sense her involuntary shivers. No longer could she rationally deny what her heart had been shouting: she was head over heels in love with Greg Delgado!

Now she understood what blues singers meant when they moaned about carrying a torch. The one Tracy carried for Greg blazed brighter with each stolen glance. From across the room, she memorized the angle of his cheekbones, the broad, strong lines of his shoulders as he worked at his desk. Knowing that he belonged to another was reason enough for her heartache. Occasionally he looked up from his work, caught her gaze, and tossed her a warm smile. The smile she sent his way was carefully calculated to disguise the churning at the pit of her stomach.

They worked together with quiet ease. His cheerfulness was so unlike the stony front he displayed during the early days of camp that even Diane was bewildered. "Tracy, what have you done to tame, Greg? He's becoming downright civil. Has the mighty tyrant fallen in love with you?"

Blushing involuntarily, Tracy responded with feigned disinterest. "Oh, Greg's in love all right, but certainly not with me. He's getting married soon, didn't you know?"

"Married! Greg? Are you sure you have the facts straight?"

"Of course I'm sure. He's building a house for his bride."

"I'm amazed that you managed to get that much out of him. Greg's specialty is stinging barbs, not small talk. You must know the formula for bringing out his good side, if there is one."

"You're too hard on him," Tracy said. "He's very kind and easy to get along with when you know him. It's true that he runs things around camp with an iron hand, but he has to because Doc hates to come down hard on people. Greg's just looking out for Doc's reputation and the good of the camp."

"Methinks you protest too much," Diane said. She sauntered over to Greg and put her elbows on the desk. "What's all this about you getting married?"

He did not take his eyes from the task at hand. "Where did you hear that?"

"From Tracy. Where else?"

"If you heard it there, it must be true," he said.

"Anybody I know, Greg?"

"Maybe. Maybe not."

Diane persisted. "Is she pretty?"

"Spectacular!"

"Brainy?"

"That too. She knows when to keep her mouth shut, a quality certain people around here lack."

"Sarcastic as ever, aren't you, darling?"

"It's the best defense against snoops," Greg said. He tossed Tracy a wink and a smile so infectious she could not help returning it, no matter that her longing was in vain and Greg's heart was firmly cemented to a faceless woman she would envy forever.

Despite her unrequited love, Tracy's professional relationship with Greg was warm and comfortable. Each seemed to know when the other needed something—a freshly-sharpened pencil, a new tube of glue, or an empty storage bin. Once when R.J. went to Greg with a problem, she heard him say, "Why don't you ask my partner over there? She can help you."

Tracy felt the knot in her stomach tighten at that. She was grateful that Greg thought enough of her ability to trust her with a technical question. Even though their tie was merely academic, she looked forward to the brief moments when they closed the lab for the evening and paused to chat about the day's work, often lingering on the porch to prolong her joy—and agony.

One evening toward the end, Greg finished before Tracy's work was done. She watched him clear his desk, stack his papers, and start toward the door. She assumed that he had gone, but when she finally turned to leave, he was sitting in the shadows at the back of the lab, his feet propped up on a desk.

She gasped. "Oh! You startled me. I thought you'd gone."

"Just waiting for you."

"You didn't have to do that. I could have closed up by myself."

"I know I didn't *have* to. I wanted to." Breaking into the smile Tracy had learned to adore, he stood up and stretched. "If you're ready, I'll walk you back to your cabin."

"But you don't have to ..."

Laughing, he said, "We've just been through that. Come on, Tracy." He took her firmly by the elbow and was about to steer her out the door when he stopped abruptly, relinquished his grip, and pulled his wallet from his back pocket. "I keep forgetting to show you a snapshot of my house. It was taken before I came up here and was still under construction, but you can get a pretty good idea of what it will look like from this."

Tracy peered at the photograph. Even under the dim light of the lab, the splendor of the house was evident. "It's gorgeous, Greg! It's like something in a magazine."

He could not disguise his pleasure. "Do you like it?"

"Like it! It's fabulous! Your girl will be crazy about it."

He returned to photo to his wallet. "I'm glad to have your approval. It confirms that the builder's on the right track."

And I'm on the wrong one, Tracy thought. The man I want belongs to somebody else. Lowering her eyes so Greg could not see the tears welling in them, she walked alongside him and listened while he talked in low, companionable tones. For a moment, she almost forgot that their life together was near an end. But the next moment she chided herself for succumbing to the charm that continued to emerge with each meeting, a sweet innocence that she concluded had been nurtured in the orphanage. She struggled to accept the fact that camp would soon close. Everyone would scatter to the four winds, Greg to his job in a distant oilfield, Iris to Boston, Becky to Bryn Mawr, and al the others to their individual destinies.

For Tracy, the prospect of becoming Doc's assistant at the university was rapidly losing its luster. She wondered how she could have been so foolish at the summer's outset to fancy herself on the threshold of a dream job. At the same time that the membership of the gem ring was yet to be resolved, her dreams—both awake and asleep—were crowded with faces and scenes dominated by Greg. Deep inside, she knew that she never could dismiss him from her mind, bittersweet though the memories would remain.

So thoroughly did Tracy savor each moment with Greg that she grew panicky as the final week began. Once the field materials were in, everyone curled up in cool, shady spots to complete their reports while Tracy and Greg brought the lab tasks under control. At length, there was nothing left to do except tag the boxes for shipment to the university museum. These would be loaded into Greg's truck the last day, ringing down the curtain on Tracy's small, sad world centered around him.

Looking back at that day, she could not explain what propelled her. She supposed it was one of those impulsive moves one makes when the world is coming unstrung and a forlorn heart refuses to accept simple logic. Her sole intention was to thank Greg for teaching her the lab procedures she would need in her new job, nothing more. She chose to confront him when nobody else was around, before the final frantic surge of camp activity tore them apart.

They had completed checking off the boxes against their list. When the last one was accounted for, Greg beamed down on her. "Congratulations to us! This wouldn't have been possible without your help, Tracy. I never thought we'd accomplish everything that had to be done."

Tracy tried to smile back, but the gravity of her mission loomed overhead. "Greg, I want to thank you for …" She stopped. The words refused to come out the way she had planned. Greg stood a mere arm's length away waiting for her to finish her sentence, but her voice faltered and she began to tremble.

His steady gaze was disarming. "You want to thank me for what, Tracy?"

She took a deep breath before plunging to the point, "… for helping me, teaching me, saving my life, and … just being my friend."

He stared at her with disbelief. "You talk as if this is the end."

"Well, it is. Isn't it? I'll be working for Doc, and you're going back to your job and your new house … and your new wife."

Tracy choked on those last words. Greg stared at her, not fully comprehending. "You're completely mistaken. We most certainly *will* see each other!"

As his mouth twisted in faint amusement, she suddenly glimpsed a far different scenario than she had first imagined. She gasped, horrified. "Oh, but we can't! It's not right! You'll be married, and … and, oh, Greg!" All the pain and sorrow and secreted love tumbled into the open. Her hands flew to her eyes, seeking to contain the torrent of tears spilling through her fingers.

Gently, Greg pulled Tracy's hands away from her face. Through the blur of tears, she saw that he was laughing. "Please, please, please don't laugh at me, Greg."

"I'm not laughing at you, Tracy, believe me." Greg drew his kerchief from his hip pocket and dabbed clumsily at the tears cascading down her cheeks. "Please stop crying and pay attention to me while I explain about …"

She heaved a sob. "You don't have to explain anything, Greg. It's not your fault, it's mine."

He put his arms around her and drew her close. "Tracy dear, nobody's at fault for any reason. There's absolutely nothing wrong. From what I see, our lives have just taken a spectacular turn for the better."

Afterward, she remembered only the way she crumbled at his touch, at the sound of his voice, and the caress of his lips on her forehead and cheek, but whatever fate had programmed to happen between them was shattered. At the precise moment their lips were about to meet, a loud crack resounded from somewhere on the other side of camp, like the ping of a stone hurled at a tin can. It was followed by muffled cries and a scream.

As one, they bolted from the lab. They dashed across the driveway, Greg in the lead, past the dining hall to a small grove of pines bordering the staff cabins. By the time Tracy caught up with him, Greg was kneeling on the ground cradling Doc's head. A few feet away, Julia, wild-eyed and shaking, was staring at them. Farther along, Snakeskin stood over Woody who was sprawled on the ground. Even as Tracy watched in horror, Julia lost her grip on the gun clutched in her hand and it fell to the ground.

Greg tossed Tracy the kerchief that only moments before was drying her eyes. "Here, Tracy! Grab the gun. Be careful. Don't get your fingerprints on it."

Tracy approached the gun gingerly, wondering if Julia would try to reclaim it, but she quickly sensed that Julia, quaking like an aspen, was unaware of her surroundings. It was absurdly easy, after all, to scoop up the gun. Tracy deposited it on the ground well beyond Julia's reach, then took the woman firmly by the arm and steered her to a low bench. Obediently, Julia sat down. Her eyes, Tracy saw, were glazed, as if in a trance.

By this time, others had heard the commotion and were running toward the scene. Enlisting the aid of Red and Joe, Snakeskin pulled Woody to his feet.

"Stay with Julia," Tracy directed Iris, as she relinquished her charge and ran to help Greg. He had ripped a sleeve from his shirt and placed it over a spot on Doc's chest. Already it was sodden with blood, the stain widening rapidly. Doc tried to raise his head.

"Don't move, Doc." Greg spoke with authority.

"I … have … to … tell you …" Doc's words were labored.

"Don't talk!"

"But … I'm … I'm …"

"I know all about it, Doc."

"Greg, I'm … your …"

"Believe me, I know. And it's all right," Greg said.

Tracy saw a glimmer in Doc's eyes. "You … know …?"

"Yes."

"How … long …"

"For years, Doc, years."

Doc smiled faintly and closed his eyes. His head jerked backward and his body gave a final convulsive twitch as Tracy's eyes darted from one man to the other. Now she understood.

"Why, you're …!" Tracy clapped her hand over her mouth as Greg's eyes flicked up and looked directly into hers. She felt curiously giddy, torn between the utter horror of the scene and delicious deliverance in knowing the dreadful secret that had been submerged for so many years.

Chapter 22

For the next thirty-six hours, Juniper Junction was buffeted by a collage of voices. From her station at the office telephone, Tracy observed a parade of officials from the university, state police, BIA agents, and newspaper reporters, all seeking details about the tragedy. She could not escape the constant deluge of their questions, the pressure from strangers on the other end of the line and the quavering voices of camp members stunned by Doc's death.

The facts, she quickly learned, were not exactly as they appeared at first exposure. Amos Green, the primary detective on the case, began interrogating Woody the moment he arrived. Descended from early Arizona pioneers, Amos inherited their no-nonsense, rough and tumble philosophy of dealing with those above the law, no matter their social standing. In short order, he cut through the knotty details to ascertain that Doc had been the brains behind the fire agate smuggling ring. Woody, abetted by Shirley, was merely his tool. While his deputies took them in custody, Amos led Julia into the office for questioning. Tracy jumped up from the desk, believing that she was in the way, but Amos waved her down.

His voice was gruff, yet kindly. "Stay where you are. You won't bother us." He pulled a tape recorder from his briefcase, and laid it on the table.

Tracy slipped back into the chair and tried to appear disinterested as Amos settled himself opposite Julia and recorded for later reference the brief particulars of time, place, and name of the detainee. She could not help overhearing everything that ensued.

"Now, Mrs. Baxter, when did you first learn that your husband was smuggling gems off the reservation?"

"I never knew that he was. I thought Woody was the only one involved."

"Really?" Amos, skeptical, drummed his fingers on the desk. "Let's begin another way. When did you suspect that something illegal was going on?"

Julia's lower lip trembled. Tracy noticed that her make-up was applied imperfectly. The Julia she met in Globe could not have appeared in such disarray. Now she spoke hesitantly, her sophisticated assurance in disarray.

"When we were at Juniper Junction last summer, I began to think that something was going on behind my back, but I had no idea what it was, only that Woody and my husband spent a lot of time conferring after hours. Sometimes Doc wouldn't get back to the cabin until after midnight." She laughed faintly. "Lucky for him, he kept fit without needing more than a few hours of sleep. I didn't want to irk him by complaining.

"After his department at the university got back to normal in the fall, things quieted down between the two men. They would meet occasionally at our home, but only in Doc's study with the door closed. I kept telling myself that my suspicions had been foolish. Once when I took them a pot of coffee, they were discussing a deal involving 'stones' as I opened the door. We were in the process of landscaping our yard, so I took that to mean decorative stones like the ones people arrange in their gardens."

Amos snorted. "It never occurred to you that it could mean precious stones?"

Julia glanced down at the rings on her hand. "Doc bought me quite a few turquoises and diamonds, but I never knew him to sell any. The idea never crossed my mind, and I certainly didn't know about the fire agates. I never knew there was such a stone until after … after this happened." She sighed and shot Tracy an apologetic look. "Apparently Greg Delgado did know about them, and he knew that taking them from the reservation was illegal."

"And that's why he was working with the government to break up the ring and learn the identity of the ringleader," Amos said.

"Greg is the most honest, dependable person I know," Julia said, without prompting. She directed her comment to Tracy, as well as to her interrogator.

Tracy said nothing, but she knew that Julia spoke the truth. She turned her head away, trying to act as if the papers on the desk absorbed every fiber of her being, yet burning to overhear the rest of the interview.

"We need to get back to the point, Mrs. Baxter," Amos said. "How did you finally learn that Doc was involved in the ring?"

"It happened after we arrived here this summer," Julia said. "I was reading a book in our cabin when I heard voices whispering outside the window. I crept in that direction as quietly as I could. It was difficult to hear every word, but I managed to make out enough to understand that Woody was hiding something in his cabin that had been stolen from the Apaches. He and Doc were talking about all the money they would get from dealers in Mexico."

"Do they say how and where the exchange would be made?"

"The best I could understand, Woody and Shirley would go to Mexico after we closed camp for the summer for a few days of vacation before the fall school term began. They would make arrangements to meet the dealers in several cities."

"Did you tell your husband that you overheard?"

"Yes. I told him as soon as he came into the cabin. He was angry at first, but as we talked, he admitted that he knew Woody was getting over his head in something illegal and had asked for his advice."

"He never mentioned that he was equally involved?"

Julia shook her head. "No he didn't. He insisted that he was on the outside looking in at a messy situation. He said the only reason he was talking with Woody is that he felt sorry for a close friend who could be in deep trouble. He told me not to worry, that he had done nothing wrong. Of course I believed him, so I demanded that he send Woody away from Juniper Junction before word got out. If anyone at the university learned that he associated with a thief, Doc would be dismissed and his reputation would be ruined."

"What was his reaction?"

The expression on Julia's face reflected her dismay. "Doc was an expert at telling a lie and convincing you it was true," she said. "He promised to send Woody away from Juniper Junction, but days passed and nothing happened until yesterday when it all came to a head."

"Go on."

"I was in the cabin when Woody came by to see Doc. I refused to let him in and told him that Doc wanted nothing more to do with him. That's when he got nasty and said there was no way Doc would double cross him because he had enough on Doc to send him away to prison for years.

"Just then, Doc came up behind me and told Woody to pay no attention to me, that I was getting hysterical about something I knew nothing about. I don't remember exactly what I said then, something to the effect that I probably knew enough to send them *both* away. Then Woody got really angry. He told Doc that I'd become too much of a problem and it was about time to get rid of me. Doc became furious. Their voices got louder and louder until both men were so enraged I was afraid they'd come to blows, so I moved away from them. The next thing I knew, Woody turned on his heels and left. Doc and I continued to argue for a few minutes until …"

Julia began to shake. Tracy read fear in the older woman's eyes.

"Yes?" Amos was impatient.

Julia took a deep breath. "We saw Woody coming back. This time, he carried a handgun, right out in the open. The expression on his face made it clear that he planned to kill someone. At first I assumed he was after me because of what I'd said to him. I'm sure Doc thought the same thing because he hurried outside to meet Woody, probably to calm him down, but the next thing I knew, Woody was pointing the gun at Doc. I heard him say that he was about to do something he had wanted to do for a long time because he was sick of being the one who did all the dirty work while Doc ran the ring like a master puppeteer. He said that he finally would reap all the rewards with Doc out of the way. Doc told him he'd better think twice, that others would turn on him."

Amos leaned forward. "So where did you come in?"

"I knew where Doc kept his own handgun. He boasted that he never used it on anything but an occasional rattlesnake. It took me only a second to decide that Woody was more of a threat than any rattlesnake. I grabbed the gun and ran outside. My intention was to shoot Woody in the arm or leg, just enough to incapacitate him. Anything to prevent him from harming Doc."

"What went wrong?"

A gasp of sorrow caught in Julia's throat. When she could speak, she said, "Doc moved."

"He moved? Why?"

"He heard me coming from behind and must have thought that Woody would make good on his first threat and shoot me. I aimed the gun, planning to hit Woody in the arm. At the split second when Doc turned around to warn me to get back, I pulled the trigger. He had accidentally moved into the line of fire. Instead of hitting Woody, I killed Doc." Julia dissolved into sobs and buried her head in her arms.

Tracy, no longer able to restrain herself, sprang from the chair and reached out to comfort Julia. That small gesture brought Julia back to the present. Striving to preserve her cool image, she patted Tracy's hand, dabbed her eyes with a tissue and drew herself up to face the next question.

With a jerk of his head and a reproving glance, Amos motioned Tracy back to the desk. Then he resumed the interview. "Do you remember what happened after Doc fell?"

"Someone came running around the corner. I think it was Snakeskin Sommerville. Yes, it *was* Snakeskin. I saw him tackle Woody and kick away his gun after it fell to the ground."

Tracy spoke up. "She's right. Snakeskin is the one who took charge and prevented Woody from doing more harm."

"But Greg is the one who really took charge," Julia said. "He deserves all the credit."

"She's right about that, too," Tracy said.

Standing abruptly, Amos clicked off his tape recorder and took Julia by the arm. "All right, Mrs. Baxter. Now that we have a pretty good picture of the scene, you can come along with me." He turned to Tracy. "If anything occurs to you after I've gone, you can contact me through Mr. Delgado."

As Amos was leading her out the door, Julia called back to Tracy over her shoulder. "Remember, Juniper Junction's greatest treasure isn't in the ground."

Before Tracy could think of anything sensible or comforting to say, Julia was gone. From the office window, she watched Amos usher Julia into the back seat of his cruiser, protecting her head from the door frame with his meaty hand. As the cruiser pulled away, churning dust in its wake, Snakeskin bounded across the path and into the office.

He doffed his hat and sprawled in the chair Amos had vacated. "There goes the witchy woman, and good riddance." He leaned forward. "Do you suppose she really loved Doc?"

Tracy nodded. "I'm sure she did. After all, she came here with him every summer even though she hated the place. She must be devastated knowing that she's to blame for his death."

Snakeskin nodded. "And no wonder. Much as I never cared for her, we now know that Doc was a Jekyll and Hyde. It would be a pity if she does time for his murder."

Tracy frowned. "That shouldn't happen. From what she told Detective Green, she was trying to stave off an attack by Woody when Doc jumped into the way. Besides, both men were in the wrong. They knew perfectly well that they were illegally profiting from mines on the reservation. Not only that, but they encouraged some people at camp to do their dirty work. In the process, they put Alice—and, for all we know, maybe some others in her village—in jeopardy by bribing them to steal gems from the storehouse."

Snakeskin leaned closer, so close that his beard dusted the top of the desk where Tracy sat. "Juniper Junction is only the tip of the gem iceberg. In time there'll be a lot more crimes attributed to Doc besides stealing gems"

Tracy bristled. "Are you quite sure you know what you're talking about? It's bad enough that he took advantage of those on this reservation."

Snakeskin looked her dead in the eye. "Doc had a way of mesmerizing folks. Apparently Woody was his right hand man in this operation, but Doc never lacked for a supply of flunkies in his department. They came out of the woodwork wherever he set up his archaeological digs, from here to Central America, just to have their names attached to his publications. In the three years I've been coming to camp, I knew that something wasn't quite right, but I couldn't put my finger on anything specific. Now it all becomes clear. I can't believe I was so dense."

"What makes you think that Doc's responsible for more crimes than the Juniper Junction gem ring?"

"I overheard Greg talking with the BIA agents. Turns out he's been working with them for several years."

"I see." Tracy saw no reason to tell Snakeskin that she, too, was aware of Greg's role, but she was pleased that others would begin to appreciate him for his determination to keep the reputation of Juniper Junction impeccable.

Snakeskin lowered his voice. "Between you and me, the best—or the worst, depending how you look at it—is that the agents told Greg the F.B.I. is looking into the theft of hundreds of ancient artifacts. Most were fenced and sold to collectors worldwide. They think Doc avoided detection by paying artisans to construct copies that couldn't be distinguished from the originals. The copies were then sold to museums with nobody the wiser."

"Except Doc and those who abetted him," Tracy said. "It's no wonder his academic colleagues were puzzled by his wealth. My professor thought it was inherited. Others probably reached that conclusion, too."

Snakeskin rose. "Now we know the truth. It's kind of sad that a single shot brought us to the end of an era. Unless another archaeologist of some renown steps forward to continue the work here, Juniper Junction will be wiped off the map. That's okay by me. I just accepted a job offer with a crime lab in California. But what about you? Weren't you planning to work with Doc?"

Tracy lowered her eyes. "To be truthful, I haven't thought about what I'll do. Obviously, I need to find something else."

"Well, you don't have to worry. You're competent enough for whatever comes along. It probably would be a good idea for you to stay in the area, though."

"Why do you say that?"

"Woody and Julia are both in custody on separate charges, although she's likely to get out on bail until her trial comes up. The way the court system operates, it'll be some time before either case is placed on the docket. And don't forget about Shirley and Brenda. They're accessories to the theft. These cases could eat up a lot of time. No matter when they're scheduled, you and I are sure to be called as witnesses, so stick around. A word to the wise, my friend."

Snakeskin clamped his hat on his head as he headed for the door, leaving Tracy to ponder the fates of the principals. More importantly, she had to make a decision that could affect the rest of her life.

Chapter 23

Through the interrogations and the tentative funeral arrangements, Greg remained calm, sensible, and thoroughly in charge. Tracy admired the way he presided with dignity while the other camp members commiserated with one another in small, quaking groups. Doc's death would have been a shock to Tracy under any circumstances; now she was faced with the fact that it meant automatic unemployment for her.

She waited for a lull in the office before placing two telephone calls. The first was to the airline. Even if Snakeskin was correct and she would be needed to testify, that could be a year or more away. If nothing else, she wanted to confer with her father. He could suggest her best course of action in the interim. At the same time, it might be helpful to see Ken and talk over the situation with him, no matter that she realized they would never be more than friends.

After making a reservation for a flight back to New York, she called Dr. Findlay to learn if her old job was still vacant. If not, she prayed that he knew of a staff position she could slip into for the fall term.

His response was quick and reassuring. The university had several slots she was qualified to fill and he promised to meet with the dean immediately to arrange a temporary position at the very least. But before she could thank him, he asked a disturbing question.

"Are you sure that returning to New York is your best course?"

"I don't know what else to do," she said.

"Have you talked to Greg?"

"Greg! You know Greg Delgado?"

"He's an old friend. If he's around, I'd like to speak with him."

"You never mentioned …" Tracy stopped in mid-sentence. She felt the hairs on the back of her neck stand up. Without turning around, she knew that Greg had entered the office. She passed the phone to him. "Dr. Findlay's on the other end, Greg. He'd like to speak with you."

"Thanks, Tracy." His expression was impossible to read.

Still stunned, she began to move away politely, but he motioned her to wait. The moment he returned the instrument to its cradle, she challenged him. "You never told me you know Dr Findlay."

Greg gave an apologetic shrug. "I never found the right moment to tell you."

She looked up at his face, studying its contours until another face tweaked her memory. "Did you ever have a beard?"

His eyes widened. He seemed on the verge of replying when one of the detectives burst into the office with some final questions before wrapping up the Juniper Junction part of the investigation.

Tracy never saw Greg alone again until late that evening. She had finished sweeping out the lab, probably the last time anyone would have that chore, she realized. By then, everyone had packed for an early morning departure. Stu and Joe finished helping load Greg's truck until there was not an inch to spare, and as they drifted away to their cabin, Greg mounted the steps for one final survey of the lab, now barren of everything. Except memories.

Snapping off the lights, he said, "That does it." His tone was commanding, yet gentle, as he added, "Get your sweater, Tracy. The temperature's dropping. I'll meet you by the dining hall in a few minutes."

When Tracy returned, Greg was sitting on the stoop, his chin resting in his hands. He's like a forlorn little boy, she thought, but when he rose to join her, the child fell away. Without a word, he took her hand and led her along the gravel trace until they reached the fork to Forestdale. There they left the road and struck out across the tall grass in the direction of the pueblo, its stones glistening like alabaster beneath the full moon. The millions of stars high above were magnified by the clear, cool desert air. Tracy almost believed that she could reach up and pluck one from the blackness. With her small hand in Greg's enormous one, she was filled with a serenity that surmounted all her troubles. Her heart was so full she could scarcely breathe. She wished she understood everything Greg was thinking.

In the hours since Doc died, Tracy had decided to savor every remaining moment with Greg. Armed with the certainty that he was her one true love, she was beset by the realization that he had other obligations and this would be their final meeting. No matter how one-sided the romance was destined to be, and how futile was the fantasy in which he took her in his arms and professed eternal love, she needed to be near him long enough to draw strength from his character. He had proved himself to be the rock Julia knew him to be. Tracy knew full well that Greg would leave Juniper Junction tomorrow to spend the rest of his life with the woman of his choice. Even though she was not the fortunate one, she would forever cherish the lessons he taught her about faith, honesty, and responsibility to others.

Upon reaching a smooth, flat section of the pueblo wall, Greg stopped and motioned Tracy to sit down. Looking back toward camp, she saw several tiny lights pricking out of the dark pines, but shortly they flicked off, one by one, and she had the distinct impression that no people remained in the world except the two of them beneath a sky so brilliant it might have been daylight. Their hands were still clasped, like sailors clutching a lifeline. Tracy became aware of electrical sparks flying between them as they studied the sky in silence. She chided herself for having an overworked imagination.

Just when she thought her heart would burst, Greg turned toward her and said, "You're the only other person in the whole world who knows."

"I should have seen it from the very first day," Tracy said.

"Was it that obvious?"

"Not at first. Your personalities are so unlike. Doc was the hail-hearty-well-met type, and you … well, you grow on one."

The sharp details of Greg's face were distinct in the moonlight. Tracy caught his brief smile as he squeezed her hand. "Am I to take that as a compliment?"

"Without question." She searched his eyes. "Nobody else knows?"

"Not a soul. When Doc first came around to the orphanage, he must have had some clue that I was there. He never claimed to be my long-lost father, just someone who liked to work with underprivileged boys. I accepted that. In fact, I never suspected otherwise until I began to mature and noticed a strong physical resemblance. Some of my pals at the orphanage remarked about it, too. And years later when he stopped by football practice at the university, guys on our squad asked if he was my father. Of course I brushed them off and explained that he was merely my advisor. At that point, it would have been painful to confront him and ask if he was my natural father, so I never did."

"That probably was the best way to handle it," Tracy said. "Neither of you were forced to feel guilty toward the other. He gave what he could by supporting your education and giving you the means to choose a career. You certainly repaid him in full. In the end, your roles were reversed and you became the one in charge. He had the fame, but you have the character. He must have been very proud of you." Greg gave her hand another warm squeeze in thanks. "But what about your mother? Why did she give you up?"

"She didn't give me up, Tracy. Without any help from Doc, she raised me until I was three. That's when she died of cancer and I ended up in the orphanage. And that's where Dr. Findlay fits in."

"I've been wondering about that," Tracy said.

"Several years ago while I was still an undergraduate, I met him at a conference that Doc and I were both attending. He was immediately interested in me because his wife's maiden name was Delgado. She had a younger sister who ran away with a man her friends described as 'a handsome, devilish stranger.' The family never met him or knew where he came from. After she left home, they never heard from her again. They concluded that she was too ashamed to return home because she was expecting a baby …"

"And the baby was you! So *that's* the connection! Did Dr. Findlay and his wife figure out that Doc …?"

"Was the cad who broke her sister's heart? I'm sure they reached that conclusion very quickly because they've been far more cordial to me from that first meeting than you'd expect them to be to one of Doc's students. The three of us never dared admit what we believed, the Findlay's probably for fear they were mistaken, and me to avoid tainting Doc's name and reputation. Since then, I've visited with them several times and have had to field a number of pointed questions. Nelly Findlay was convinced right away that my mother and her sister were one and the same, and when I showed them her picture, that was enough proof for her."

"And what about the resemblance between you and Doc? Did they give any hint that they suspected him?"

"They never came right out and asked me if I know my father's identity, but when I was describing how we first met and all the ways he's helped me, I saw them exchange knowing glances. They're well aware that Doc was a rolling stone emotionally, not like these strong ones all around us that have been here for centuries."

"As charming as Doc was, he was very deceitful," Tracy said. "Now that I can look at him objectively, I'm amazed that he was able to get away with so many evil actions over such a long time."

"His demise says it all. It pays to be truthful no matter the consequences. Which brings me to confessing that I haven't been completely honest with you, Tracy."

"What do you mean?"

"It's about my girl …"

"Oh." Tracy felt as if she were in an elevator plunging to earth.

"… the fictitious one."

Tracy caught her breath. "Fictitious? I don't understand. You said …"

"I said very little, Tracy. If you think back, you picked up on a casual remark and gave it substance."

Tracy marked his shy grin. "Then … you're not getting married?"

"You're misinterpreting my words again. Listen carefully: Tracy, *you* are the only woman in my life."

"I am?"

"Can't you tell?"

Tracy shook her head, trying to stem the tears of happiness.

"I guess I'm no good at expressing my feelings," Greg said. "I thought you knew how much you mean to me. Until everything fell apart, I expected you to stay in Arizona. Now that you're leaving, well …" Greg's voice broke imperceptibly. "I suppose you've made a sensible decision, but … do you mind if I come to visit you at Christmas time?"

"Mind? I'd love it!"

Greg beamed. "There's a geology society conference in New York at the end of December. If I arrive a few days early, we could spend time together."

"Can you be there for Christmas Day?"

Greg dug his boot in the dirt absently. "I don't want to interfere with your family's plans."

"Oh, but you wouldn't! Their plans go on without me. You see, Dad has remarried and I'm sort of in the way, like excess baggage. I'd so much rather spend Christmas with you, Greg."

"You would?" He broke into an enormous smile. "Well, then, could we have a tree? It's silly to admit, but I've never had one of my own, and …"

"Oh, you poor darling!" Tracy cried. "You will have a tree with all the trimmings, and lots of presents, and … oh, Greg! Won't it be wonderful!"

Before she finished speaking, they were in each other's arms. As Tracy nuzzled his shoulder, she saw one star, then another, hurtle down across the heavens, and she wished … wished …

Greg stroked her hair awkwardly. "Tracy dearest, don't you think it's about time I kissed you properly?"

Her head shot up and she looked him squarely in the eye. "Greg Delgado, if you *don't* kiss me this very moment, I'm going to take matters into my own hands. The very idea of you wasting more of our precious time by asking such a ridiculous question when every time I turn around I find myself in your arms wishing you'd do something about it, but thinking you won't because you belong to somebody else, and I've been absolutely heartsick! If I'd known better, I wouldn't have let you waste so much time …"

"Quiet woman! Now who's wasting our precious time?" Without another moment's delay, he kissed her soundly.

The love and understanding flowed back and forth between them so fiercely that Tracy knew she was home at last.

"Christmas can't come soon enough," Greg said, just before he kissed her again.

Chapter 24

Upon awaking the next morning, Tracy had a brief spasm of fear that the previous evening had been a dream, but the reality kicked in when she saw Greg waiting for her outside the dining hall with the same fire in his eyes that had been blazing when they kissed good night. They walked slowly, cherishing their last few moments together and allowing the others to scurry past them into breakfast. Tracy knew the time would be brief because she, along with Becky and Iris, were leaving camp with Ray and Marie. Ray would drop them off at the Phoenix airport for an afternoon flight. Her pounding heart dulled her appetite for anything other than strong, black coffee.

"Please eat something, Tracy," Greg said, after watching her refuse every platter passed down the table.

Her voice dropped to a whisper. "It's the company. My stomach's filled with butterflies."

Sternly loving, he said, "My order. You have a long day ahead. I don't want you to waste away before I see you again."

Tracy allowed him to spoon some scrambled eggs onto her plate and managed several bites before Ray clapped a hand on her shoulder. "Come on, Tracy. I have to load your things in the station wagon now or we'll never make that flight."

The kitchen crew, eager to close up the building and return to civilization, had already begun to clear away the tables. Haste was foremost in the minds of everyone. Cabins were stripped clean, trucks packed, and cars loaded.

One by one, the groups left camp, Snakeskin pulling out first, followed by the Psi Theta boys. Clarence and the kitchen crew were shuttering the dining room as Ray hustled Tracy into the back seat of his station wagon, saying, "Let's go! I can't drive fast over these roads."

They pulled away in a skirl of dust. Tracy's face was pressed against the window for a glimpse of Greg. She knew he was making the final rounds of the camp buildings after checking out Clarence and the kitchen crew. She kept looking back, hoping to catch a glimpse of him, but he was nowhere in sight.

They had not traveled beyond the first bend in the road when her tears began to fall softly. Job or no job, Greg was all that mattered to her now. In his arms, she felt secure and loved. And yet the ghosts persisted. Mentally she went over every word, every gesture from the previous evening and realized that he had not yet committed himself, *really* committed himself beyond a visit at Christmas time.

As the rugged miles between them lengthened, Tracy found herself shifting responsibility from Greg to her own timidity. All her life, she had avoided confrontation, never quite able to seize the moment forcefully. Now her lack of courage was being tested and she was the only one able to rise to the challenge.

Suddenly her role became clear. She saw that her decision to leave Arizona was her way of punishing herself for all that had happened at Juniper Junction. Greg must have realized that, too, for by letting her go, he had passed the responsibility to her for making the next move.

She, after all, was the only one capable of righting a terrible wrong. The answer lay in her heart and the words within that were pleading to be released. Greg had never heard those words spoken by another living soul. Now it was her duty to speak them and set free the little boy in the orphanage who clung tenaciously to the wisp of a fragile dream in which he loved and was loved in return.

"Ray, stop the car!"

Marie's head snapped around. "Have you gone mad?"

Ray peered at Tracy through the rear-view mirror, snorting in disbelief. Iris and Becky stared, open-mouthed.

"Now what?" Ray was visibly annoyed.

"Please let me out. I must wait for Greg."

"Here?" Marie's voice jumped an octave. "Why would you want to wait for Greg?"

Marie's reaction confirmed to Tracy that she and Greg had not become a camp item. "Because I have something important to tell him." She struggled to project calmness. "Now if you'll just dump out my things, you can hurry on your way so Iris and Becky don't miss their plane."

Iris looked mystified. "How will you get home?"

"I've decided to stay in Arizona," Tracy said.

Marie frowned. "But what about a job? Doc was your main contact."

"I'll find one. I'm not worried. There are lots of things I can do."

Convinced that Tracy was serious, Ray brought the car to an abrupt halt. Before allowing her to have second thoughts, he unloaded her trunk and set it by the side of the road.

Marie continued to fret. "I'm worried about you, Tracy. What if Greg doesn't come this way. He could take the road to Springerville, instead. It's longer, but not as hilly. He may decide that's a better choice considering the load he's carrying."

"He'll come." Tracy spoke with a defiance she could hardly recognize.

But her optimism began to wane as she watched the curls of dust disappear down the road. The longer she waited, the more frantic she became. The possibility Marie brought up had never crossed her mind. Greg *might* choose the level route. Then what would she do? She tried to think positively. Sooner or later an Apache cowboy was bound to ride by; she hoped that would happen before she collapsed from heat exhaustion.

Tracy judged that she was about ten miles from camp. It was too far for her to think about retracing the route without her canteen, the one she had thoughtlessly packed in the trunk. Empty. Furthermore, she was not even dressed sensibly for walking. The tailored dress and heels she had chosen for her assault upon civilization were totally inappropriate in the wilderness. Furious with herself, she sank down on her trunk and expended her frustration by idly digging into the dry soil with a stick she found lying near her feet.

Like many archaeologists who admit to having "feelings" about certain sites, Tracy was inexplicably attracted to the tiny plot with nothing to recommend it other than its proximity to an ancient trail and a metallic rim protruding imperceptibly along one edge. At first she believed it to be a hub cap hurled from a passing truck, but as she bored into the soil with her stick, a curious outline began to emerge. The longer she toiled over the small excavation, the more excited she became. She dug relentlessly until the moment the thrumming calm was broken by the hum of an approaching engine. Expelling her emotions in a sob, she leaped to her feet.

The load in Greg's truck lunged and shifted as he slammed on the brakes, killing the motor. He jumped from the driver's seat and stood in the road gaping while the dust swirled and churned around them. "Tracy ...?" His voice was thick with awe.

"Oh Greg, I was terrified you'd taken the other road."

"How … how did you get here?" He did not budge. The distance between them loomed as daunting as an enormous gulf.

"I asked Ray to let me out. I couldn't go back."

Something in Greg's eyes tugged at Tracy's heart. His hat was in his hands. Slowly and mechanically, he turned it around and around, waiting for her to continue. A lock of hair had fallen across his brow. In a flash, amidst the eerie vacuum of the settling dust, Tracy received the vision of a small boy standing in the courtyard of an orphanage waiting for someone, for someone who never would volunteer more than a token of the love the boy craved. And yet that boy accepted the love offered on meager terms. Now, intuitively, Tracy felt a mystical connection with an almighty being, one that had anointed her with the power to give that boy all the love he had been denied. The moment had come to transport the cold, secret vault of his life into the blinding sunshine.

Already the sun had ascended the sky and penetrated the pines standing sentinel-like along the track. Tracy took a step forward and began to speak, slowly measuring every word. "I love you, Greg. It wouldn't have been any good going back because I would have been thinking of you every moment and aching to be with you. And as for waiting until Christmas to see you, I … I couldn't even have waited until Halloween." Her nervous laugh was matched by a faint smile curing across Greg's lips. "Courage and integrity were just words until you taught me their true meaning. All I ask of life is to spend it with you." In a very small voice, she added, "If you'll have me."

"If I'll have you …?" Greg's voice cracked, and for one bleak second, Tracy felt absurdly brazen. But her fear evaporated on the wind as Greg moved with the speed of a crazed beast and swept her into his arms, murmuring, "My darling Tracy, I love you, love you, love you!"

After they had kissed and clung, and laughed and cried together, and spoken those endearing phrases that cement lives, he said, "My dearest darling, do you know why I'm late?" Wordlessly, Tracy shook her head and snuggled deeper into his arms. "Because I can't live another day without you," he said. "When I realized that you were actually gone, I couldn't bear it, so I called the airport and asked them to hold you there until I arrived—to marry you."

Tracy giggled deliriously. "You did that? Would they have stopped me from boarding?"

"The people I talked with were very sympathetic. I'm sure they would have done all in their power to hold you there, but just in case something went wrong, I called Dr. Findlay and told him he might have to meet you at the airport in New York and keep you safe until I caught a flight. Now that you're here, we don't have to plan for those complications. As soon as we deliver this load to the museum, we'll head to the courthouse and apply for a marriage license. At the next stop, we'll pick up our wedding rings. How does that sound?"

"It sounds as if my guardian angel deserves a bonus," she said. "In the past few weeks, I've learned how to open my heart, even though I was afraid that it was in vain."

"You'll never have to wonder about me, Tracy. Doc and I are romantic opposites. I'm what you anthropologists call a thoroughly monogamous man, and I picked you out for my mate a long time ago."

Tracy drew back. "What ever do you mean by that?"

His eyes twinkled. "With a little bit of help from Dr Findlay."

"Aha! I've smelled collusion since that phone call the other day."

"You have a sharp nose," he said, giving it a loving peck.

"Well, go on," she said, laughing.

"Very well, my sweet. Two years ago while I was back East for a conference, Dr Findlay and I were chatting in his office when you dropped by to hand his secretary some papers. Even though you didn't notice me at all, I was bewitched the minute I saw you. I was so flustered, I declined when he offered to introduce us, but this past spring when I learned that Doc planned to hire an assistant, I got brave and asked Dr. Findlay to submit your name."

"But I found the announcement on the bulletin board. I told Dr. Findlay about it, not the other way around."

"Our plan worked perfectly. He tacked it up trusting that you'd take notice."

"You're a fine couple of conspirators. And that takes us back to yesterday."

Greg laughed. "And a belated answer to your question. Yes, I *did* have a beard until the day before you saw me in Phoenix. It's not easy to shave every day when you're working out in the oil fields."

"So! You *were* the man in Dr. Findlay's office when he told me about the job. And I saw you there other times, but never suspected a thing."

"One and the same. I'd have taken you in my arms just like this, then and there, if you'd let me."

"Not very likely."

He grinned. "Both Nelly and Dr. Findlay said you'd be a tough customer. That's why I had to go about winning you carefully."

Tracy ran her fingers through his hair, savoring his nearness. "But what if it hadn't worked out? What if I hadn't fallen in love with you after all?"

"That was a chance I had to take," he said. He brushed his lips against her cheek.

Just before he kissed her again, Tracy said, "Thank goodness you did!"

Dozens of kisses later, Greg stood back to survey Tracy. "I don't know about you, but I'm ready to put this place behind us and get on with our lives. How about it, love?"

"Not quite yet," Tracy said.

Greg looked a question. "Not yet?"

She tugged at his sleeve. "Darling, come with me. I think I've found something terribly important." Her excitement mounting, she drew him over to her small excavation which, by now, revealed the crown of a helmet. Although tarnished, it was unmistakably silver. Greg let out a long, low whistle. "Is it …?" Tracy began.

Before she could finish, he confirmed her suspicions. "Spanish! I wouldn't be surprised if … wait here!"

Turning on his heels, he fairly flew to the truck. Momentarily, he returned with a shovel, a trowel, and a brush. Tracy, transfixed, watched him scoop clods of earth from around the perimeter of the depression, then manipulate the brush until the visor emerged. Deftly, he worked around the metal headpiece to avoid damaging the skull below. At last, the conquistador's helmet stood free.

Still kneeling on the ground, Greg tested the soil at several locations along the burial, probing with the trowel until he heard the clink of another chunk of metal. Without speaking or taking his eyes from has task, he held out his hand. Tracy's field training jumped to the fore. Automatically, she passed him the brush and knelt down beside him. She watched, scarcely breathing, as his hand, shaking almost as much as hers, whisked away the last few grains of soil covering a magnificent Spanish cross. Centuries of internment had done nothing to subdue the gleam of rich gold. The jewels—rubies, emeralds, and diamonds—dazzled beyond belief.

Greg sat back on his heels. "You've done it, my dear! Found us a real Spanish grave!"

So as not to disturb the Iberian ghosts, Tracy whispered, "What does it mean?"

"It means that Coronado and his men passed this very way in search of the Seven Cities of Cibola. They never found the gold they were seeking. Instead, many died during the journey. This is the grave of one."

"What ever do you imagine his companions were thinking to bury such valuable jewelry with him in a remote spot like this?"

"They were honoring the teachings of their culture," Greg said. "Their religion was very important to them, almost as important as their craving for gold. The Spanish explorers were also superstitious. Historical records confirm that they brought members of the clergy along on all their expeditions as a buffer against harm by the native people they believed were heathens. In addition, every man wore his own cross for protection, some more elaborate than others. Because the cross represented the individual's relationship with God and his promise for salvation in the hereafter, the survivors felt obligated to leave them with the owners."

"That's logical," Tracy said.

"Another reason why they were so cavalier about discarding ornate crosses like this is that they expected to steal enough gold from the Indians to make their own valuables look insignificant."

"But in the end they didn't find any gold."

"Not a drop. It was all part of a beautiful legend, as ephemeral as life itself. Which is why I intend to make every minute count from this moment forward." Greg rose purposefully and pulled Tracy up beside him. "As soon as I take some photographs, I'll cover up this site and we can be on our way."

Tracy waited while Greg captured the scene on film with his camera. "Do you suppose that this is the only Spanish burial in this location?"

"It could be. Or maybe an illness slowed down their progress and they lost several men at the same time. We'll never know until there's an official study approving excavation of possible sites. He's been here more than four hundred years, so a few more months or even years *in situ* won't hurt. In the meantime, these photographs will be proof that you and I aren't hallucinating."

"Shall we report the grave to the museum?"

"Let's sleep on it," he said. At Tracy's reaction, he broke into laughter and planted a kiss on her forehead. "A figure of speech, sweetheart. To answer your question, we should tread softly at first. This is a project the university might pursue if they keep Juniper Junction as a research site, but with Doc gone, that will be up in the air for quite a while."

"Wait a minute, Greg! We've come beyond the boundaries of Juniper Junction. This land is on the reservation, so it's government property. The university won't have the authority to disturb it unless they negotiate for the access."

"You make a good point. Since the legal owner is either the Apache tribe or the United States government, the courts would have to decide. That could take decades. For my part, I'd like to see this tribe reap the financial benefits. Certainly there should be plenty. They could use some good luck, poor souls."

Tracy nodded eagerly. Their minds were so in tune, it was uncanny! Then she had an awkward thought. "Greg, do *we* have a claim on it, since we found it?"

"That's the third possibility. If it turns out that we do have a legitimate hold on it, Tracy, would you want to come back here sometime in the future to dig for additional treasures?"

She shook her head. "Maybe when everything is settled and the unhappy memories have faded I'll be more enthusiastic, but for now I'll be content to live a normal, peaceful life with you."

Greg grinned. "My sentiments exactly. Well, señor, we'll tuck you in again," he told the bones beneath the surface as he began shoveling the soil over the helmet. "You can continue dreaming your impossible dreams while mine are coming true."

Tracy regarded him tenderly as he flashed her that wonderful smile, the smile of a man who knew he was adored. And presently, Tracy and her love climbed into his truck to begin the journey to their future.

EPILOGUE

Tracy caught her breath. As Greg and Jason, their strapping youngest son, jumped out of the car and bounded up the ridge to the pueblo, she had a fleeting vision of Doc and a younger Greg hovering over her on this dig site so many years before. She returned their wave, puzzled at first by her family's sudden return from Forestdale, but a quick glance at the sky confirmed that twilight was descending. She had been sitting on the wall and daydreaming longer than she realized.

Tracy owed this day to Jason, an aspiring architect. Although she and Greg often spoke about visiting Juniper Junction, the occasion never arose until Jason's curiosity about primitive engineering prompted them to make arrangements the next time they returned to their base near Phoenix, the home Greg built so many years ago in the Superstition Mountains. While their three children were growing up, Greg's career with a major oil company took the family to exotic places around the world, from the sands of Arabia to the steppes of Russia. For Tracy, none of the natural wonders they viewed during their travels compared with the beautiful memories of the brief summer she spent at Juniper Junction.

So it was that they entered the reservation armed with a permission slip granted by the tribal headquarters, unaware that a paved road reduced the travel time to just over a half hour. The original journey to Juniper Junction took ten times as long. Upon reaching Juniper Junction, they found a thriving Apache settlement stretching from the small original community to the former camp site. The dining hall, classroom, and infirmary had been converted into homes, the cabins turned into sturdy storage shelters.

The poverty of the Apache village Tracy remembered was replaced by a visible prosperity. Never could she have imagined that the tribe's wealth would come from the opulent casino they had passed before turning off the main highway instead of the range cattle, the fire agate mine that was still untapped commercially, or the Spanish treasures which the tribal chief declined to unearth years earlier when Greg showed him the photographs of the conquistador's grave.

Greg, understanding the chief's decision, stowed the photographs in the old trunk he had carried to Juniper Junction. "Human lives are too sacred to exploit," he told Tracy.

The secret was theirs to keep.

Despite the changes man had made on the reservation, the magical aura of the sweeping prairie and the eternal mountains remained. Unchanged, too, was Greg's warm smile. As he reached the crest of the rise and approached Tracy, their eyes locked. Their minds converged.

Jason, right behind him, broke into their reverie. "Forestdale's a great example of primitive structures, Mom. You should have come along. Dad and I didn't see a single snake."

Tracy laughed. "No thanks. I'm willing to trust that adventure to you two. Besides, I wanted to spend time here. This is the most special place in the world to me."

Greg turned to Jason. "It represents a summer of your mother's time and energy, but its greatest fame is as the ancient site of our first kiss."

Jason grinned broadly. "So this is where it all began. I guess I owe my existence to Juniper Junction."

"You and your brother and sister," Greg said.

Tracy smiled. "The shooting stars did the trick. Since everything I wished for that night came true, it's safe to give them credit."

Jason, amused, quietly contemplated the sight of his parents gazing into each other's eyes, their arms entwined. At length, he said, "You're the best. While we were growing up, there were times when we were embarrassed to see you two acting like a couple of teenage love birds, especially in front of our friends, but it paid off. Megan and Josh are both happily married, and I know your example will rub off on me when I find the right girl."

"That's the most a parent could wish," Tracy said. "Scientists have learned volumes about early man, but each generation has to discover and cultivate love from scratch."

"There's one basic rule you need to learn, Jason," Greg said, tossing Tracy a wink. "Let your sweetheart know at the earliest possible moment how you feel about her. Your mother once accused me of making her cry all night because she thought I was in love with someone who didn't exist."

Jason's eyes widened. "Is that true, Mom?"

"I'm guilty, but your father put my mind to rest on this very spot. That's why it's so precious to me. A woman needs assurance that she is loved."

"And so does a man." Greg said, slipping his arms around Tracy. "How about it darling, shall we relive our first kiss?"

Tracy lifted her face to his. "Greg Delgado, don't you dare waste time asking."

When she finally caught her breath, Tracy said, "Even better than the first."

"The credit goes to the many happy years of practice you've given me," Greg said, his eyes twinkling, and he kissed her again.

Tracy was still savoring the kiss when she remembered. Her lips brushed his ear as she whispered, "Greg, I just saw Julia."

He drew back, surprised. "Julia? Julia Baxter?"

"I'm sure it was Julia. You might not have noticed, but before you dropped me off, we passed a roadside memorial. When she drove up and got out next to it, I recognized her walk. Except for that gorgeous auburn hair turning white, she's changed very little, even after all these years."

"A memorial! Was it …?"

"Yes, I'm sure it's for Doc. When I got my bearings, I realized that the new road goes right past where their cabin was located. Look down there."

Greg shaded his eyes from the setting sun, still intense as it sank beyond the hills. "When I stood on top of the broadside I could look right down at the men's cabins. And you're right. That must be the exact spot where he fell." He grasped her hand. "Before we leave, let's pay our respects."

They hurried down the rise and across the field to the road. Upon reaching the memorial, Tracy saw that Julia had surrounded it with pots of geraniums.

"That was a lovely choice," she said. "Red stands for love and geraniums bloom for months in this climate. But why do you suppose she erected a memorial here? His actual grave is miles away."

Greg shook his head. "That's hard to say. She dropped out of sight after Woody went to prison. For all we know, she may live nearby."

"This is the last place the Julia I knew would have chosen to settle down."

"Time is a great healer of sorrow and of silly notions," Greg said.

"It also draws you even closer to the ones you love. Julia must have really loved Doc."

Tracy heard the catch in Greg's voice as he said, "Despite his many flaws, I did too."

"And he truly loved you, Greg. He could have deserted you forever, but in time he realized that his duty was to honor his obligation. As you grew into the sort of man he admired, he handed over his most important responsibilities to you. Not many fathers have sons like you."

Greg leaned over and kissed her. "You're slightly prejudiced, but I'll accept the compliment my love. However, I must point out that not many parents have children like ours." They kissed again, this time with renewed passion until the blare of the car horn brought them around. "If I'm not mistaken, one of them is becoming annoyed with us."

Jason, at the wheel, leaned out of the window. "Hey, turtle doves! It's a long drive home. When I'm back at school, you'll have the house to yourselves."

"Now there's a son who knows how to get his father's attention," Greg said.

"And his mother's too," Tracy said, as she slipped her hand into his.

Laughing merrily, they ran to the car and settled themselves for the ride home. As Jason gunned the motor and pulled away from Juniper Junction, the ghosts of the past retreated silently through the pines.

978-0-595-41164-1
0-595-41164-9

Printed in the United States
139714LV00003B/16/A